PAWSITIVELY POISONOUS

A Witch of Edgehill Mystery

Book One

MELISSA ERIN JACKSON

Ringtail
PRESS

Ebook ISBN: 978-1-7324134-3-6
Paperback ISBN: 978-1-7324134-6-7

Front cover design by Maggie Hall.
Stock art via Designed by Freepik, iStockPhoto, Shutterstock.
Interior design and ebook formatting by Michelle Raymond.
Paperback design and formatting by Clark Kenyon.

First published in 2019 by Ringtail Press.
www.melissajacksonbooks.com

To Sam

CHAPTER 1

The palm-sized black toy lay curled on the countertop. Amber stood on one side of the counter, the other swarmed by the wide-eyed, upturned faces of six little boys and girls, their parents forming a wall behind them. Some looked as delighted as their children. Others, especially the fathers, appeared nothing short of harassed—all folded arms and pursed lips.

Amber supposed she couldn't blame them for being skeptical and a bit wary during her toy demonstrations. They watched with dubious concern, not trusting the toys and trinkets their children brought home from the Quirky Whisker. The toys that seemed to move on their own, that played with their children for hours without showing signs of slowing down. Toys that couldn't be dismantled to replace the "batteries" when the toys inevitably stopped working in a year or so.

By way of explanation, she would say, "Oh, they've got tiny computer chips inside that power them." And, "I can't explain how they work, exactly! The designs are perfected by an engineer who wishes to remain anonymous."

Besides, with their fickle, ever-changing focus, the children would lose interest in the toy in question soon enough, and her creation would languish in a box or under a bed or in the back of a closet, gathering dust. The spell would have worn off

1

by the time the old toy was rediscovered; it would be immobile and unresponsive, as if its battery had finally been drained.

Then Amber would have a new toy on the market and the children of Edgehill would beg their parents to replace the ones they'd already abandoned.

"Are you ready?" Amber asked now, bent at the waist with her arms resting on the wooden countertop so she was eye level with the kids. Her dark brown hair hung over her shoulder in a loose braid, the ends gently tickling her arm.

She got a wave of nods in response.

Her attention shifted back to the black plastic toy, this one fashioned to look like the curled, sleeping form of a cat. Its tail was wrapped around its body, hiding its paws.

"Wake up, little one," she said softly, placing a single finger on one of the cat's pointed ears, before pressing down.

The tiny plastic ear gave a click and sank into the cat's head before popping back into place. Amber folded her arms on the countertop again, giving the toy space. The cat's head lifted then, blinking slowly, to the delight of the watching children. The toy cat's back faced her, but she'd seen the cat perform its tricks dozens of times, perfecting the act before she'd invited the kids to see it.

The plastic cat blinked its round green eyes a few more times, then yawned, its tiny fangs visible as its pink tongue stretched out a few centimeters. The kids giggled.

Childlike wonder in the form of wide eyes and slightly agape mouths usually overtook the parents at this point. And, as expected, the expressions on all the parents' faces, save for one, lit up at the sight.

Owen Brown never smiled during a demonstration. Amber wondered why he continued to show.

The cat rose to all fours, hoisting its butt in the air as it stretched, tail curled overhead like a miniature cane. Then it plopped down on its haunches, tail wrapped around its feet. The tip flicked periodically.

The children erupted into applause, turning quickly to their parents to tug on shirts and pockets and purse straps, pleading for another of Amber Blackwood's unique toys. Amber straightened, smiling to herself.

Owen Brown's young son turned back to Amber when his parents began a whispered conversation about whether or not they truly needed another one of these things. "Miss Amber? What else does the kitty do?" he asked, keeping his voice low.

Amber rested her arms on the countertop once more, the wood smooth and worn from years of use. "Can I show you something special?"

The little boy, if he stood on tiptoes, was just tall enough to get his nose to clear the surface. She saw more of his mass of curly blond hair than anything else. That mop of curls bounced as he nodded.

"I programmed this one to obey a couple commands. It will only work for a very special owner, though, and won't work for anyone else," she said.

Amber had started adding voice activation "technology" to the toys only recently—the spells involved had been particularly tricky to master.

His blue eyes widened. "*Me?*"

"If you want, I think I can get Midnight here to listen to you."

The toy cat, now named Midnight, Amber supposed, had been sitting as still as a statue—save for the occasional flick of his tail—but turned his head at the sound of his new name and blinked a slow cat blink at the little boy.

The boy grinned, showing a missing front tooth. "Hi, Midnight. I'm Sammy."

A tiny mew echoed from the plastic cat. The little boy giggled again, eyes bright.

Amber's gaze shifted to the other children and their parents for a moment, but no one seemed to be paying them much mind.

Owen Brown's attention flicked away from his wife and toward Amber then, a scowl drawing his brows together. Certainly, he hadn't heard the meow from the cat, had he?

Two of the kids had grown bored and darted off toward the toy display on the other end of the store. The floorboards creaked under their tiny feet as they ran. When Amber's attention shifted back to Owen, he was talking to his wife again.

Amber shook it off. But, just to be sure, she mentally uttered a spell of secrecy and gave a slight flick of her wrist. Neither the cat nor Sammy seemed to notice.

"Now, Sammy," she said, looking at the little boy as he tightly gripped the edge of the counter, focus squared on the cat. "Midnight here is like a dog—he knows 'sit,' 'come,' and 'roll over.' All you have to do is say his name and give the command."

Sammy's eyes somehow widened further. After a long pause, he said, "Do I do it right now?"

"Mmhmm."

Sammy's mouth bunched up on one side, and his brows pulled together. Utter concentration. He looked like a miniature version of his father. "Midnight, come."

The plastic cat stood on all fours, then walked over to Sammy, got right up to his face, and sniffed his nose. Sammy squeaked and let go of the counter to clap his hands. "Midnight, roll over!"

The cat lowered itself to the counter, all four limbs bunched as if prepared to spring from the wood like a cricket, but then froze.

"What ... what happened?" Sammy asked, grabbing hold of the counter again. "Did I say it wrong, Miss Amber?"

Just then, a hand landed on Sammy's shoulder. "How much is this one going to set us back, Miss Blackwood?" his father asked.

She straightened. "Well, since this one is the demo toy, it's only five dollars."

Owen squinted at Amber. She could tell him it was a lovely day and he would still look at her as if she'd just admitted to some heinous crime. To say she felt like he didn't entirely trust her would be an understatement.

Of the year.

Amber figured police chiefs were naturally distrustful, having seen the worst humanity had to offer over the course of their careers. Owen had spent most of said career in bigger cities, namely Portland. Moving to Edgehill three years ago had no doubt been an abrupt change of pace for him, but given the hard-edged stare he angled at her—oh, all the time—she knew his Spidey-police-senses hadn't been left behind in Portland.

Those senses clearly went into overdrive around her, even though he hadn't a clue why.

Amber flicked a glance at his wife standing nearby, silent as usual. The woman had a hand on her very pregnant belly.

Without a word, Owen fished a five-dollar bill out of his pocket and dropped it on the counter. Shoving his wallet into the back pocket of his jeans, he ruffled his son's hair. "Let's go, Sam. We've got to get your mother home and off her feet."

Owen and his wife, Jessica, headed for the door.

Abruptly, Midnight tipped to the side, rolled, and popped back onto his feet. Then he went back to his default sitting position. Sammy let out a squawk of joy.

"Remember," Amber said, "the commands will only work for you ... no one else. No one else will ever be able to see his tricks." She scooped up Midnight and placed him in Sammy's waiting, outstretched hands.

The boy tightly clutched the toy to his chest. "But you saw him do it."

"I'm his mom, so to speak, so I can see it, too," she said. "Just you and me, kid."

Sammy grinned his gap-toothed grin. "Thanks, Miss Amber! I'll take real good care of him. I promise!"

Amber watched as the boy went bounding out of her shop after his parents.

Twenty minutes later, the shop was empty again. Five other toy cats had been sold—at full price—along with Midnight, and Henrietta Bishop had purchased her weekly batch of "sleepy tea."

Henrietta was a middle-aged divorcee who'd moved to

Edgehill specifically to embrace the "Crazy Cat Lady" lifestyle. She was a lithe redhead with a mass of curls that hung to her mid-back. They never were truly contained, no matter what she did. Currently they were loose and out of control. She reminded Amber of the girl from the Disney movie *Brave*.

"I really wish you'd tell me what you put in this stuff," Henrietta had said for the four hundredth time, affectionately patting the bag with the Quirky Whisker's logo on it—a bespectacled and top-hat-wearing cat with a wealth of whiskers spreading out from his smirking face. Amber's younger sister, Willow, had designed it.

"A girl never tells her secrets," Amber had replied, as usual.

"Works better than melatonin! I swear you need to sell this stuff online. You'd make a killing. Works like magic!"

If only Henrietta knew.

Now it was just after ten in the morning and Amber was blissfully alone. With any luck, this would hold out until noon when she closed for an hour for lunch.

She busied herself with tidying up after the tornado of children that had torn through. The toy section had super-bouncy balls and plastic animals scattered on the ground, knocked off the kid-accessible lower shelves. One of her favorite plastic dragons lay on its back, red wings flush with the floor, tiny taloned feet pointing toward the ceiling. The dragon looked mildly embarrassed, lying on her back when she was meant for the air.

Picking the dragon up, Amber laid the creature in her palm, wings outstretched and talons resting on Amber's skin. With a soft, "Scarlet, fly," the dragon toy came to life and pushed off from Amber's hand, soon wheeling around the dreamcatchers hung from the ceiling in the dream section of the store.

Amber knew she was getting more and more bold with the toys. Her first batch had only walked on their own. Then they had walked and sat and pretended to sleep. Then she'd added voice activation. And now some could perform actions as complicated as flight.

Customers like Owen Brown were suspicious. They couldn't possibly know she was a witch, but they knew something was off in the Quirky Whisker. The more she created meowing plastic cats and flying dragons, the more likely it was that she'd be found out.

But her magic needed an outlet. Resisting the energy that thrummed beneath her skin was a surefire way to drive a witch to madness. Just a little release here and there wouldn't hurt anyone. Plus, seeing that bright-eyed look of wonder on Sammy's face had been worth it.

That was what magic was about. Wonder.

After an impressive series of loop-de-loops and corkscrew diving maneuvers, the dragon gave a tiny roar before wheeling around to head back to her. It knew as well as she did that the flight spell would only last a few minutes, and if it ran out before the dragon was somewhere safe, she'd crash to the ground.

Amber held out a finger and the dragon landed on it like a trained falcon. Amber had just returned her to her perch on top of the toy display—still as could be, once more—when the chime above her shop door tinkled, causing her to whirl around.

Immediately worried her new patron had seen her dragon's trick, this one not bestowed with the same failsafe as Midnight, she mentally went through the simple memory erase spells she knew—the kind that wiped away a small memory, no more than a minute old.

Her friend Melanie Cole walked in. Well, more like shambled in. Melanie's dark hair was plastered to her forehead, her tanned skin pale. She wore an oversized long sweater over sweatpants, and her feet were shoved into ratty fur-lined boots. In short, Melanie looked a hot mess. Melanie, who usually *never* looked a hot mess, had been battling a persistent illness for weeks.

All thoughts of spells flew out of Amber's head.

"Mel! Are you okay?" Amber asked, even though the answer was clearly no, and hurried across the creaky floors to her friend's side, wrapping an arm around her waist. "I thought the remedy you bought last week finally cleared this up. You look terrible."

"You really know how to talk to a lady."

Amber huffed, placing the back of her hand to Melanie's forehead.

"Oh, stop fussing," Melanie said, though there was no malice in her voice. She had enough strength to gently push Amber away. "I'm all right. I have a slamming headache, though. What you got for me this time? Your stuff is better than anything at the drugstore."

Amber pursed her lips, staring at her friend as she held herself up by resting a hand on a free-standing pyramid-shaped bookshelf.

"I'm all right, Amber," Melanie said again. "Stop being a worried grandma and go get me the good stuff."

Amber harrumphed but hurried behind the counter where she kept her tinctures and teas.

Melanie made a slow shuffle toward the counter. "No more tea, though. I'm so sick of it. If one more person brings me tea, so help me ..."

"Okay, okay, no tea," Amber called over her shoulder, laughing softly. "Where's that boyfriend of yours? Shouldn't he be feeding you chicken soup and giving you foot rubs?"

The back wall had been designed to mimic an old apothecary shop—sturdy shelves holding various herbs and liquids in glass jars took up the top rows, while the bottom rows—from floor to waist height—were made up of drawers.

"I'm *still* not talking about him," Melanie said. "Stop fishing. None of the fish are biting."

"Am I going to have to wait until your wedding to know the guy's name? Assuming I'm even invited ..."

"Guilt won't work either, poppet," Melanie said in a fake British accent. "Things are going good, though. I'll tell you that much. I think he's finally ready to take this to the next level. But that's all I'm going to say! I don't want to jinx it."

Sighing, Amber gave up. She knew she could always magic the information out of her friend one way or another, but that never felt right. Amber hated to use her magic to manipulate others; she wasn't the type to exploit her powers for personal gain. She was a Blackwood, not a Penhallow, after all.

White cards adorned with Willow's crisp, clear handwriting had been slipped into slits on the face of each square drawer, labeling them with an ailment or focus.

Acne, bug bites, cardiac, dreams ... she moved further

down the alphabet. Gallbladder, hangovers—ah, headaches. Amber trundled the drawer open and pulled out one of the small glass vials, this recipe heavily featuring passionflower, which would help Melanie's headache.

With her back turned to Melanie, Amber muttered a quick activation spell—causing the ingredients to work twice as fast—and waved her hand over the vial. Then Amber turned to face Melanie, who now had her arms folded on the counter, her head propped up on one hand. Her eyes were closed. Had she fallen asleep?

"I think you need to see a doctor, Mel," Amber said softly.

Melanie gave a start and opened her bleary eyes, but righted herself quickly, placing her hands on the worn wood of the counter to help push herself to standing. "Just need a little rest." Jutting her chin toward Amber, she said, "That it?"

Amber glanced down at the label-wrapped vial in her hand. The tiny bespectacled cat of her logo eyed her from the space between her fingers. The label read, "For headache treatment, add this to your favorite beverage, or drink directly for more immediate relief," and stretched long-ways across the thin tube. "Any other symptoms? Can I get you anything else?"

Melanie shook her head, her brown hair hanging limply around her shoulders. These last few weeks, Amber's friend looked worse than she'd ever seen her. Melanie had lived in Edgehill for just under two years, but she'd quickly wormed her way into everyone's hearts with her charm and humor. Her looks hadn't hurt either—better suited for runways and magazine covers than a small Oregonian town best known for its annual cat festival.

Amber handed the vial to Melanie and went over the instructions for their use, despite being printed clearly on the label. "This one has a bit of valerian root in it. It'll knock you out so you'll sleep deeply—just don't take it until you get home."

"You're a love," Melanie said, slipping the vial into the small purse slung over her shoulder, then starting to root around for something.

"If you're looking for money, just stop," said Amber. "I'm not taking a penny from you. My payment is you getting better, okay?"

Normally, Melanie would have put up a fight, but she gave in immediately. That was how Amber knew her friend was truly unwell.

Walking to the other side of the counter, Amber wrapped her arm around her friend and guided her to the door. "Can I walk you home? Call you a cab?"

"Stop fussing," Melanie said. "I'm going to chug whatever foul thing is in that magic vial, and I'll be back to my old self by morning. It's just a bug."

"A very persistent bug that leaves and comes back. Repeatedly."

Disentangling herself from Amber, Melanie turned to face her and patted Amber's warm cheek with her cool, dry hand. "Don't worry about me, okay? We'll have lunch next week to talk more about the festival. I've been getting questions left and right about those toys of yours. Maybe we can double your profits from last year—we'll discuss numbers."

Well, Melanie couldn't be *that* sick if she was saying things like "discuss numbers." Melanie lived for numbers.

The chime tinkled again as Amber pulled open the door. Melanie stepped out, huddling a little deeper into her oversized sweater as a gust of cool wind whipped by.

"Don't drink that before you get home," Amber reminded her. "And don't mix it with any other medications."

"Yes, *Mom*," Melanie said, some spark coming back to her tired brown eyes, her ashen lips turning up in a small smile. "Thanks again, hon!" she said as she walked out into the cool January morning, waving a hand over her head as she slowly made her way up the sidewalk.

If only Amber had known then that those were the last words she'd ever hear her friend say.

CHAPTER 2

At noon, Amber locked the front door of her shop from the inside and pulled down the sign hanging against the glass. The sign's back was made of a light-colored wood, the front modeled to look like a chalkboard. Next to the bespectacled cat logo etched in white chalk were the words, "Open! Please come in!" written in cheery cursive.

Placing the sign on her flattened palm, she flicked a furtive glance out onto Russian Blue Avenue. The street was always quiet around noon, as several of the more popular cafés, restaurants, and coffee shops were a block away. Sure no one was watching, Amber waved her free hand over the surface of the sign.

The bespectacled cat who, just moments before, had been tipping his hat in greeting, now held up his watch-wrapped wrist, the "finger" of his other paw pointing to the gleaming clock face. The letters changed their message to, "We'll be back at 1 p.m.!"

Amber hung the sign, cat facing out, back onto the hook attached to the door. The wooden corners of the sign tapped gently against the glass as it settled itself on its burlap strap.

She changed up the sign display every few weeks, mostly for her own amusement. Customers must have thought she either was particularly skilled with chalk or had a box of ready-made signs at her disposal.

Amber headed for the door at the opposite end of the shop, marked "Employees Only." A narrow set of stairs, arching toward the right, led to her tiny studio apartment above the store. As she walked, she pulled the tie from the end of her hair and unwound her braid, shaking her hair loose and letting it fall past her shoulders in dark brown waves.

She was halfway up the creaking staircase when the agitated, low yowl of her cat, Tom, sounded from above. The orange-and-white tabby sat at the top of the steps, eyes squinted in mild annoyance, the tip of his striped tail swishing. He'd been her inspiration for Midnight the toy cat.

"I'm right on time, you glutton," she told the gorgeous, svelte feline. "You won't starve in the time it takes me to get up there and fill your bowl."

Tom Cat yowled and swished his tail again, clearly not believing her anymore now than he ever had in the past.

Once she was one step from the top, Tom bounded away on silent feet to the other end of her tiny studio apartment, where she'd set up a little cat nook for Tom and Alley. Every day at noon, he ran to his bowl as if he needed to guide her there, lest she forget where the object of his life's passion resided.

Alley, a black-and-white cat with a splash of black covering half of her face, lay curled at the foot of the bed. She only stood and stretched once she heard the *clink, clink, clink* of her kibble hitting her bowl beside Tom's. Tom had already scarfed down half his food before Alley delicately jumped to the ground.

Having quieted Tom, Amber fixed herself a turkey

sandwich, which she then took to her window bench—her favorite spot in her apartment. The door to her shop was just below her. Beyond that was the stretch of Russian Blue Avenue. Then Birman Drive, Bengal Way, and there, off in the distance, was Ocicat Lane. The street she'd grown up on.

The house—what was left of it—still stood there. Renovations had begun a few months after the fire that had killed her parents. Aunt Gretchen had come in from Portland to help take care of the legal matters. Gretchen was her father's sister—a woman Amber and Willow had only seen on major holidays. But shortly after the fire, when Amber had been sixteen and Willow fourteen, Aunt Gretchen had swooped in, instantly becoming a life raft in their sea of grief. Amber didn't know what they would have done had it not been for Gretchen. The sisters had no other family—at least no one who hadn't shunned the small family of Blackwoods. All Amber knew was that, years ago, some offense had resulted in the almost total alienation of her small family of four. Drama didn't escape witch families any more than did it human ones.

Gretchen had rented out her place in Portland and moved to Edgehill so the girls could finish high school. They'd lived in an apartment building spitting distance from the hulking, charred remains of Amber's childhood home. She'd had to walk past it every day on her way home from school and could see it from her bedroom window as she drifted off to sleep at night.

Now, fourteen years since her parents' death, she could still see the unfinished house from her window and was reminded every day that if she and Willow hadn't stayed at a friend's house that night, maybe the sisters' magic could have saved their parents.

"*Or perhaps you would have died in that fire, too,*" Gretchen had often told Amber, usually after Amber had woken from a nightmare, screaming and thrashing and beating away flames. "*Maybe you were spared.*"

Amber ate her lunch in silence, staring at the house out on the far horizon. The house Gretchen had sunk thousands of her savings into in hopes they could restore the building to its former glory. But one day, shortly after Willow's eighteenth birthday, Gretchen had suddenly called off the workers. She'd begged Amber and Willow to just forget about Edgehill, with its heartbreaking memories, and to come back with her to Portland where they could start anew.

Amber had always wondered where the abrupt change in her aunt had come from.

She suspected it had something to do with the fact that Willow had received an acceptance letter to her art school of choice just days before. Amber knew her sister wanted out of Edgehill just as much as Gretchen did.

But Edgehill was the only home Amber had ever known. The place that held all her memories, good and bad. She couldn't imagine ever leaving it. She couldn't as a twenty-year-old, and she couldn't now, a decade later.

Tom hopped onto the window bench, pulling Amber's attention away from the view out her window. Tom began licking Amber's discarded plate, lapping up any crumbs he could find. She grabbed him, settling him in her lap. He relaxed against her with little protest and tucked his paws under his chest, purring contentedly. They sat like that for a while, Amber's mind blissfully blank as she stared out at the clear, cloudless sky.

Movement down on Russian Blue Avenue caught her eye and she saw Betty Harris opening her bakery—Purrfectly Scrumptious—across the way from her own shop. Betty flipped her sign over, unlocked the door, and propped it open with a rock. It was chilly in Edgehill in January, but the scents wafting out of Purrfectly Scrumptious were more than enough to bring people in. Betty's shop cat, Savannah, a fluffy gray-and-white Maine Coon, sauntered out and then promptly flopped over onto her side. Savannah pulled in just as many customers as Betty's delicious cakes and cookies.

The sight of Savannah meant Amber's lunchbreak was nearly over.

Standing while still clutching the purring Tom to her chest, she deposited the cat onto her bed beside the already-dozing Alley. Tom turned in a couple of circles, much like a dog, and curled up next to his sister.

Amber had just reached the top of the stairs when her house phone rang. It was such an ancient relic, but the people of Edgehill were big on their landlines. Which was just as well, as Amber was terrible at remembering where she'd last left her cell phone. Nothing a quick locator spell couldn't fix, but still.

Plucking the phone out of its receiver, she said, "Amber speaking."

Answering a call without the input of caller ID was truly living life on the wild side; anyone could be on the other line.

"Oh my God, Amber, hi."

It took a moment for Amber to place the voice of the frantic-sounding woman. Kimberly Jones. She and Amber had gone to high school together, though they hadn't traveled in the same circles. Nothing as cliché as Amber being the weird loner and Kimberly the popular cheerleader.

No, Kimberly was just … excitable. Someone who always sounded breathless, like she was imparting the most important news the world had ever known. It was only tolerable in small doses. Once, in high school, Kimberly had come rushing over to Amber in between classes, all heavy breathing and darting glances down either end of the hallway. The girl had put a hand to her chest, large green eyes wide as saucers as they'd scanned Amber's face. Amber's heart rate had spiked, sure Kimberly was going to tell her she'd just caught Amber's boyfriend making out with a teacher … or something as equally traumatic.

"Oh my God, Amber, hi," she'd said then too. "I … oh my God. Do … is there any way … I'm so sorry about this … but can I borrow a pencil? I can't find mine and I have a math test next period."

Amber had almost fainted with relief.

A week later, however, Amber's boyfriend *had* been caught making out with someone else, so perhaps Kimberly's presence had been a harbinger of bad news.

"Hi, Kim," Amber said now. "What's up? I don't have that basket ready for the raffle yet. I'm putting the finishing touches on one of the toys. Melanie and I are—"

"Oh!" said Kimberly. "Oh, sweetie, that's … that's just it … Melanie is …"

It sounded like the other woman was fighting off tears.

Amber's brow creased. "Kim? *Kimberly*. What's wrong? What about Melanie?"

"Oh my God, Amber," Kimberly said again. "Melanie's dead."

It felt as if someone had just punched Amber in the gut, the breath leaving her in a whoosh. "What? How ... she was just here a couple hours ago."

"I know," Kimberly said, definitely crying now, the words coming out like a choking gasp. It took her a few moments to compose herself. "I went over to her house to check on her because she's been so under the weather lately, you know? She was supposed to meet me around now to discuss the raffle, and she usually calls to confirm, but I haven't heard from her since last night. She didn't answer her phone when I called her earlier."

"And Melanie always picks up."

"Right!" said Kimberly. "Her door was unlocked when I got there and I let myself in and ... oh God, Amber. She was lying in the middle of her living room, not moving. I thought maybe she'd just collapsed, but when I shook her ... she just felt wrong. Her eyes were glassy and staring at nothing and ..."

Kimberly completely broke down then.

Amber, tears in her own eyes, gave the woman several more moments to get herself under control. The word "dead" kept echoing in Amber's mind. It was so final. Amber could hardly process what it meant. "Did you call the police?" she finally asked.

"Yes," she said, sniffing. "That's partly why I called you."

Brow creased, Amber said, "What do you mean?"

"Well, when I found Melanie, one of the vials from your shop ... it was *in* her hand."

"Well, yeah. I gave her something to help her sleep," Amber said, realizing too late that a hint of defensiveness had crept into her voice.

"Oh, I'm not blaming you for anything!" Kimberly said, sounding a touch hysterical. "It's just that Owen Brown showed up and seemed very, *very* interested in the fact that something from the Quirky Whisker was found on her ... on her body. He said something like, 'Well, color me surprised,' but said it like he wasn't surprised *at* all."

Amber reeled again, as if physically struck by this news too. "He ... what? He thinks my tincture is what caused ..." Amber could scarcely complete the thought, let alone say it out loud.

Kimberly loudly blew her nose. "Let's just say I heard him say he wanted the vial bagged for evidence and he planned to interview you himself."

Amber groaned.

"I just thought you'd want to know," Kimberly said. "I imagine getting news that your friend died is bad enough, but to have Owen Brown, of all people, come swaggering in to not only break the news, but to accuse you of ..."

It seemed Kimberly couldn't voice the thought out loud either.

"Thank you," Amber said.

A loud pounding sounded below.

"Oh crap. I think he's already here," Amber said. "We'll ... we'll talk soon, okay? I can't process this right now and

I wasn't even the one who found her." Amber softened her tone. "I'm so sorry, Kim."

The other woman began crying in earnest now.

Another booming set of knocks reverberated downstairs. Amber flinched. She didn't need this right now. Her friend was dead and she needed to *think*.

"Take care of yourself, hon," said Amber, before hanging up with Kimberly, who was still so emotional she couldn't reply. Amber knew her own tears were coming; she could feel them at the back of her throat.

Dead.

How could she be dead?

Taking the stairs at a jog, Amber opened the door at the bottom of the landing and let herself into the shop.

Sure enough, Chief Owen Brown, in full uniform, stood across the way outside her door, hands on his hips, stance wide. He peered at her through the glass, his expression some combination of smugness and anger. There was no way this conversation would go well. Amber could whisper a quick spell and send him away, making him forget why he'd been here in the first place. The spell never lasted longer than an hour, especially without being in physical contact with him while the spell was cast, but it would give her time to breathe. To think. To process the fact that the once-bright, vibrant Melanie Cole who had walked through Amber's door hours before would never be able to do so again.

Amber stopped halfway to the door, hand to her stomach. Her friend was dead.

How could she be dead?

Owen Brown pounded on the door again, the sign tapping against the glass with the force of it. The jerk couldn't give her a moment's peace? Now it was her turn to be angry. No matter how strange Owen thought her wares were, how odd he thought *she* was, he couldn't possibly think she was capable of this. Of hurting Melanie on purpose.

Her anger that he could even *consider* such a thing dried her threatening tears and strengthened her resolve. She stood tall and marched to the door, unlocked it, and pulled it open.

"Hello again, Chief Brown," she said. "Something wrong with Sammy's toy cat?"

Owen stalked past her and into the store, gaze swiveling this way and that as if he'd never been inside it before. It was nearly a full minute before he finally turned to her and said, "Your friend Melanie Cole was found dead in her home an hour ago."

The words hit her like blows to her chest. She fought back an involuntary choking sound—a noise that reverberated from some place deep inside her. Her eyes welled with tears, but she clenched her jaw, willing them not to spill down her face. How dare he come here to throw something like that at her with no tact, with no regard for her feelings? She wouldn't let this man see her cry. Besides, no matter how she reacted, she knew he would find a way to deem it suspicious.

"But you already knew that, didn't you?" he asked.

"Yes. Kimberly Jones called me just before you got here."

A vein in his temple twitched. Ha. He'd been hoping to catch her off guard with the news and was clearly upset Kimberly had beaten him to the punch.

He reached into his pocket and held out a plastic zipped bag with a vial in it. One of her vials; the bespectacled cat logo on the label looked at her from the corner of one eye, appearing just as concerned about his current predicament as Amber was. "Can you tell me what this is?"

"It's one of mine," she said. "If it's the one you found in Melanie's hand—Kimberly told me about that, too—it's the headache tonic I gave her this morning."

"And what's in this so-called … headache tonic?"

He said the last two words as if they were synonymous with "poisonous snake venom."

"The ingredients are on the label," she said. "Would you like me to read them to you?"

That vein in his temple twitched again. "I'd like to hear it from you directly, Miss Blackwood."

With a sigh, she said, "Passionflower and valerian root are the main ingredients. There are some trace amounts of vanilla for flavor."

"And when did she purchase this from you?"

"I gave it to her this morning when she came in complaining of a headache," Amber said.

"*Gave* it to her," he said. "So there's no record of a transaction taking place?"

"No," said Amber. "Her payment to me was to get—" Throat suddenly tight, Amber willed the tears back. Willed her anger to return so she could get through this conversation and get this man out of her shop so she could grieve in peace for her friend. "Her payment was to get better."

"I see …" he said, tucking the bag back into his pocket.

"Were there any other customers in the shop at the time who can back up your story?"

Amber sighed. "No, it was just us."

"I see," he repeated. "I'll be sending the vial to Portland to be analyzed so we can find out just what Miss Cole ingested."

"Good," Amber said. "And when you learn what's in it, you'll see that every ingredient is natural."

"Just like those toys my son keeps bringing home."

Amber pursed her lips, a thought niggling in the back of her mind. "Why are you here? Is there something suspicious about her death? You seem to have immediately jumped to the theory that something was done *to* her, not that this was an unfortunate incident. She'd been sick on and off for weeks."

"That's not something I can discuss with you at this time, Miss Blackwood. This is an ongoing investigation."

Yeah, an investigation that had begun all of an hour ago. Was Chief Brown frothing at the mouth over Melanie's death because he was desperate to find something concretely wrong he could connect Amber to, or was he missing the fast-paced life he'd had in Portland where potentially mysterious deaths had surely happened on a daily basis?

An idea struck her.

Knowing said idea was a terrible one, she closed the distance between herself and Owen in five quick steps and placed a hand on his arm. She felt the heat of his skin through his long-sleeved shirt. "Was Melanie's death not an accident?"

Though she'd need skin-to-skin contact to be able to hear a person's last thought replay in her head, she mentally uttered

25

the incantation all the same. A flash of images popped into Amber's mind and she staggered back a step, flinching.

Owen snatched his arm toward his body, holding his elbow as if she'd singed him. No one could feel the effects of a thought-spell, so she knew Owen was reacting to her flinch, not anything she'd done directly to him.

Lip curling slightly, he said, "Like I said, it's an ongoing investigation. I cannot discuss details of the case with you." He straightened, tugging the sleeves down on either arm so the cuffs rested comfortably at his wrists. "I'll be in touch again soon, Miss Blackwood."

With that, he sauntered out of her shop without another word.

When Amber was sure he was gone, she doubled over, tears flowing freely. She held onto the counter to keep herself upright, but her wracking sobs soon took her to her knees. She rested her head on the floor, body heaving.

Not only had her friend died, but that flash of images unknowingly supplied by Owen—like a short series of crisp crime-scene photos—had been of blue-tinged lips and nails.

Amber had known in that moment what had happened.

Melanie had been poisoned.

CHAPTER 3

Amber sat with her back against the counter, legs folded beneath her. With her eyes closed, she took slow, calming breaths. When she heard the tinkle of the bell above her shop door, she let out a soft, involuntary groan. The winter months were slow in Edgehill. It wasn't until the trees grew their leaves, the flowers blossomed, and the temperature shifted from cold to chilly to warm that tourists started to venture to the feline haven that was Edgehill.

After the scheduled toy demonstration that morning, Amber hadn't anticipated any more customers today. She didn't want to fake niceties on the day her friend very possibly had been murdered.

Something hard thumped lightly against her knee. Giving a start, she opened her eyes to meet the steady gaze of a Maine Coon. Savannah bumped against Amber's knee once more, gave a soft chirp, and flopped over onto her back in front of Amber's crossed legs.

Savannah's front paws flopped on top of her chest, her expression clearly saying, "Go on. You know you want to."

Amber sniffed and gave a watery laugh before burying her fingers in the long, soft fur on Savannah's stomach. Savannah squinted her eyes closed and turned her purr on full force.

A few moments later, Amber heard, "How you holding up, hon?"

Continuing to rub Savannah's belly, Amber looked up to find Betty Harris standing nearby, one arm propped on a pyramid-shaped bookshelf stocked with guides on herbs, gardening, and crafts. Betty was an African-American woman in her mid-sixties, her hair cropped short. Her eyes were as bright blue as Savannah's.

Amber managed a half-hearted shrug, then refocused on the purring Maine Coon.

"I saw that grouchy old Owen Brown over here earlier," Betty said. "Was he giving you trouble?"

Knowing Betty likely knew as much as she did at this point—Edgehill might have been behind the times in some ways, but the rumor mill ran faster than the Wi-Fi down at the Purrcolate coffee shop—Amber told Betty about her run-in with the chief, and the fact that the man seemed to have a very short suspect list, with Amber herself at the top.

"What hogwash," Betty said, clucking her tongue. "I've known you since you and Willow were babies. I knew your parents quite well—God rest their souls—and you're one of the last people I'd ever think capable of such a thing. I don't know why that man has always turned his nose up at you."

Amber sighed. "Thanks, Betty."

After a moment, Amber still massaging the purring Savannah, Betty said, "You need anything, baby? I know you and Mel were close."

"All I want to know is who did this to her," Amber said. "Melanie never hurt anyone."

Betty made another clucking sound, softer this time, and Amber's fingers stilled in Savannah's fur. The cat gave a light trill of protest.

When Amber cocked an eyebrow at Betty, the woman shook her head. "No. I'm sorry. I shouldn't have said anything. It's not my business."

Betty hadn't actually *said* anything, but that clucking tongue of hers was sometimes more informative than words could ever be.

Savannah scrambled to her feet then, quickly padded across the shop, presumably to the spot where Amber always kept a small bowl of water and a couple treats out, should one of the town's cats drop in for a visit. While most people in Edgehill had pet cats, there was a large population of strays who lived in town. For some reason, the stray cats of Edgehill had always been friendly. No one knew why the cats congregated here. But instead of shooing them away, Edgehill's founders had built a town around them.

"Betty …" Amber said, standing and taking a couple of steps forward. "Do you know something?"

Betty pursed her lips and crossed her arms. "It's not my place. And it's just a rumor, really. Not right to spread rumors about the poor girl on a day like today. Even if it *is* true." She held up her hands, placating. "And I'm not saying it is."

Amber sniffed, rubbing the heel of a hand against one of her eyes. She was sure they had to be a puffy mess by now. "Please tell me. If it'll help figure out who might have hurt her …"

Betty huffed out a breath. "This is all speculation, mind you. I can only go by what little I've heard."

Amber managed a small smile. "Betty, c'mon. We both know you hear more gossip than a hairstylist. You lure them in with Savannah's baby blues and then get them so hopped up on your sinful cupcakes, they'll tell you anything."

Betty never backed down from a compliment. "I do have the best cupcakes in town."

"Try in the *state*."

After a moment, Betty asked, "What do you know about that man Melanie was seeing?"

"Not much," Amber said, surprised she hadn't thought of the mystery man again until now. "I just know they met on a dating site and were apparently getting serious. He lives over in Marbleglen."

Betty clucked her tongue at the name of Edgehill's rival town. Most Edgehill residents felt ... strongly about Marbleglen. It was mostly civil, like fans of rival sports teams. But the smallest slight could set off the wrong person in seconds.

Amber had once seen a bar brawl break out between an Edgehill citizen who had casually said the Here and Meow Cat Festival was exceedingly superior to Marbleglen's Floral Frenzy Flower Festival, held every year around the same time. The next thing anyone had known, the two men had been rolling around on the ground, throwing blows and colorful insults, after one of them had splashed an entire pitcher of beer in the other's face.

"Well, that's the thing ..." said Betty now, pulling Amber back into the conversation. "Most people thought that ... that he was some guy from the next town over. But I've heard from at least two reliable sources that she was seeing ... oh, I don't know if I should say this ..."

"Betty …"

"It was Derrick Sadler." Betty winced.

It took a second for that information to organize itself in Amber's head. "But he's married!"

Betty knowingly rose her eyebrows. "Hearsay."

Amber folded her arms, thinking. Derrick's wife, Whitney, had been on the Here and Meow Committee *with* Melanie. Melanie had been voted in as the festival director for this year. Whitney had continued on as the finance chair for the fourth year in a row. Amber herself was on the committee as head of the festival's design, but really, she was just the mouthpiece for Willow, who worked on everything from afar, emailing Amber with mockups for flyers, posters, and the like. Willow worked in Portland as a graphic designer at a small advertising firm.

When the festival was a couple of weeks out, Willow would join Amber in Edgehill to help in a more hands-on way. Hands-on meant that Amber and Willow would magic their way through several tasks that would take a normal human twice as long to complete.

Amber tried to think of the countless interactions she'd seen between Melanie Cole and Whitney Sadler and not one struck her as even remotely suspicious.

"Amber, dear?"

Snapping out of her thoughts, she glanced up at Betty, who now had Savannah rubbing against one of her pantlegs. "Sorry," Amber said. "It's just … it's hard to believe Melanie would be— *had* been—keeping a secret like that."

Betty nodded. "Just a rumor."

Savannah chirped.

With a smile aimed down at her cat, Betty said, "You hungry?"

"I'm guessing she already cleaned me out of treats," Amber said.

Savannah sauntered toward the door.

Betty laughed. "I guess that's a yes." After pulling Amber into a quick, tight hug, Betty held her out at arm's length. She smelled like sugar. "I'm just across the way if you need anything, okay? Even if it's just to talk. I'll whip you up some of those coconut cream cupcakes you like so much."

Amber nodded slightly. "That sounds great."

"All right, hon," Betty said. "I'll come check on you soon."

Amber watched as Betty and Savannah left the shop, the chime tinkling as the door clanked shut behind them.

Had Melanie truly been having an affair with Derrick Sadler? Derrick and Whitney had always seemed happy, but Amber wasn't naïve enough to believe that all outwardly happy couples were happy in private, too. Who knew what the realities were inside the Sadler household. Or what lies—or truths—Derrick had told Melanie about the state of his marriage.

A committee meeting was scheduled for three days from now. Amber had never talked to Whitney much beyond things directly related to the Here and Meow.

On Friday, Amber planned to get to know Whitney Sadler a little better.

In a move both self-serving and rooted in sympathy, Amber called Kimberly Jones on Friday morning to ask if she wanted to ride with her to the Purrcolate for the bi-weekly festival meeting. She knew Kimberly had to be out of her mind with anxiety after last night's town hall.

"Oh my God, Amber, thank you for calling," Kimberly answered breathlessly when Amber offered to drive. "I have most of Melanie's notes and access to her spreadsheets—she sent me copies of everything—but there's so much to do!"

"I figured," said Amber. "Maybe you need an assistant now, too."

Kimberly laughed semi-hysterically. "Are you volunteering? Because I accept!"

"Oh, I'd be a terrible assistant," Amber said. "But maybe one of the other ladies who've been doing this for a while will be able to help you. I wouldn't hesitate to ask for help; everyone will understand."

"Okay, yeah, you're right," she said. "I just need to center my chi."

After a long pause, filled mostly with Kimberly's breaths, Amber said, "So should I come pick you up at six?"

"Oh my God, Amber, yes please," she said. "You're an absolute doll."

Amber wasn't, though. Amber was a sneaky, sneaky witch who had been obsessing over the possibility that Melanie had been having an affair with a married man. Under normal circumstances, Amber might have turned her nose up a little at the fact that her friend had been partaking in infidelity, but in *these* circumstances, Amber kept wondering if Melanie's secret affair had anything to do with her death.

Which was why Amber sat idling outside of Kimberly's

house at 6 p.m. on the dot, with two steaming cups of hot chocolate—Kimberly's favorite. Amber fired off a quick text to let Kim know she was out front.

Amber's mind drifted to last night, when Mayor Deidrick had called for a meeting specifically about the festival, wanting to gauge the town's reaction to keeping the Here and Meow running as usual despite Melanie's tragic end. Though it had only been two days since Melanie had been found dead, the rumor that her death had been the result of foul play had already made the rounds.

Business at the Quirky Whisker was slow during the winter months anyway, but Amber couldn't tell if it was the brisk weather that had kept many customers from gracing her shop's doorstep over the last couple days, or Owen Brown's suspicions about her.

During the town hall, some called for the Here and Meow to be postponed until the killer was apprehended, while others felt the festival should continue full steam ahead because that's what Melanie would have wanted. Even the small contingent of Dog Lovers United had chimed in, making their yearly plea to turn the festival into a joint canine and feline event but, as usual, they'd been shut down. Many thought it was in poor taste to suggest a drastic change to the festival Melanie had already put so much work into.

Eventually, it was decided to keep things running as planned, and that Kimberly should take Melanie's place, since she'd been Melanie's assistant. Kimberly had joined the mayor at the front of the room to a series of cheers and applause, but she'd been so pale, Amber had wondered if she was going to pass out.

The front door to Kim's house opened now and Amber watched her hurry across the driveway, loaded down with a laptop bag and what looked like two purses. She pulled the passenger-side door open and practically flung herself inside, bags piled in her lap. Slamming the car door shut, Kim threw her head back against the headrest and let out a long, gusty sigh as if she'd just run a marathon.

Amber eyed the out-of-breath brunette and hid a smile. Kimberly really hadn't changed an iota since high school. Amber held the cup wrapped in a protective cardboard sleeve out to Kimberly.

Kim perked up at the smell of chocolate and turned toward Amber. "Oh my God, Amber, you really *are* a doll. Is this … is this *your* hot chocolate?"

"You better believe it."

Kimberly squealed excitedly. Disentangling herself from the various straps draped over her thin frame, Kimberly let the bags fall between her feet on the floor and grabbed the cup, placing her nose by the little spout and inhaling deeply. "Oh! You even sprinkled it with cayenne pepper!"

"Of course. I never forget an order."

Amber's hot chocolate was often a top seller during Halloween events.

Kimberly took a swig of the drink and let out a dreamy sigh, melting against her seat. "This is perfect. Thank you."

Amber took a sip of her own hot chocolate before placing it in the cupholder and pulling out onto the road. Though they were meeting at a coffee shop, Amber had known Kimberly wouldn't be able to resist her hot chocolate.

Which meant Amber could guarantee that the tonic she slipped into Kimberly's drink would be ingested without a problem. Amber felt guilty, but if anyone knew about Melanie's potential affair, it was Kim. Amber hadn't wanted to berate the woman with questions on the drive, running the risk that Kim would think Amber had offered her a ride solely to pump her for information—which would have been the truth. Instead, the tonic would make sure Kim believed she'd willingly told Amber everything she wanted to hear.

Sneaky, sneaky witch.

Assuming the tonic had been mixed properly, that is. It wasn't as easy to test out a gossip tonic as it was to work out the kinks in an animated toy. For tonics, one needed guinea pigs. And Amber's best guinea pig had moved to Portland to work in advertising.

Kimberly took another sip of her hot chocolate. "Oh, this is so good, Amber. I know it's a seasonal drink and no one wants to drink hot chocolate in, say, summer, but this stuff is absolutely to die—"

When Kim abruptly stopped talking, Amber shot a quick glance at her to see her bottom lip shaking.

Knowing Kim was now mentally chastising herself for her choice of words, Amber said, "Melanie had such a sick sense of humor—I bet she would have thought that was funny." Slipping into an impression of Melanie, she said, "*Oh, that's real classy, Kim!*"

Kimberly sputtered a laugh. But she sobered quickly. "I really miss her."

Amber nodded, chest tight. "Me too."

A charged silence filled the car.

To get to the Purrcolate coffee shop, one only had to take a straight shot down Ragdoll Way from Kimberly's house. Amber had roughly ten minutes before they reached the place *and* before the tonic wore off. Lampposts slowly started to click on as it grew darker.

They passed two small churches, a bank, and a drug store before Amber spoke again.

Taking a deep breath, she said, "You two must have really gotten to know each other well once you became her assistant."

"Oh yes! We talked nearly every day—sometimes more than that."

"I see. I wonder if … no. I …" Amber made a show of hemming and hawing over her next statement. She attempted a Betty Harris tongue cluck, knowing she didn't have the older woman's skill. But it was enough to get Kimberly's attention.

"What?"

"I just … did she ever tell you about that guy she was seeing?" Amber asked, hoping she sounded more like a playful gossip than an interrogating busybody.

But Amber needn't have worried; the gossip tonic had kicked in.

"Oh my God, Amber, I'm so glad someone finally asked! I've been dying—oh my God, I did it again!" She let out another semi-hysterical laugh. Amber made a mental note to put a little less kava in her next batch. "But ... okay, you didn't hear this from me, but she was seeing Derrick Sadler!"

Amber offered a gasp that she hoped wasn't too over-the-top.

A soft rain started to fall and Amber turned her windshield wipers onto the slowest setting. The lights of Edgehill—rectangles of warm yellow spilling onto lawns and sidewalks from people's living rooms, the bright neon blue and white of gas stations and convenience stores, the red of stop lights—grew blurry as the rain fell, then were swept back to clarity with the swipe of her wipers.

"I know, right?" Kimberly said, taking another long swig of her drink. "Our sweet Melanie, getting all tangled up with a married man. She totally didn't want me to know—for *anyone* to know—but one night we'd been working late on festival stuff. After I left, I had to double back twenty minutes later because I forgot my phone charger.

"I went up to the front door to knock and glanced into those windows right by the door, you know? And what do I see? Melanie pushed up against the wall with her legs wrapped around Derrick's waist. I was gone for less than half an hour and they were already going at it! They should have at least closed the blinds."

"Did she see you?" Amber asked, still shocked that she'd had no idea about this side of her friend.

"Well, I sort of yelped," said Kimberly, wincing. "Melanie heard it. She saw me standing there with my mouth hung open. I bolted to my car as if *I* had been the one caught in a very compromising position with a married man, and she came running after me. We sat in my car and she cried and cried and said she knew it was wrong, but she loved him and he was planning to leave Whitney ..."

"*Really?*"

"Mmhmm," Kim said. "But ... well, she told me that six months ago. Doesn't seem like he was in any real rush to leave his wife. Why give up a good thing when he can get a little extra on the side?" Kimberly gasped. "That was a horrible thing for me to say! Maybe he was planning a slow exit. I don't know. She begged me not to tell anyone. I'd never seen her cry so hard."

Amber pursed her lips. Melanie had lied about every aspect of her relationship with the mystery man. And it had been going on for over *six* months?

"Part of why she was so upset was because she said Whitney is really controlling of Derrick and that if Whitney found out about the affair, she'd—" Kimberly clapped a hand over her mouth. When she lowered her hand again, she said, "You don't think ... you don't think *Whitney* had anything to do with what happened to Melanie, do you? Oh my God, Amber, should I have told someone about the affair? Should I tell the police?"

Amber definitely needed to recalibrate her gossip tonic—it wasn't one of her strongest recipes. Plus, with tonics that coerced a person into actions they normally wouldn't take, sometimes there were adverse reactions. Such as crushing guilt.

The other woman started to hyperventilate.

"Hey," Amber said, glancing over at Kim and reaching across the center console to gently rub the other woman's arm. "Hey, just breathe, okay?"

They'd just driven by the tiny video game store, so they were almost at Purrcolate. She just needed to get Kim there before she lost it.

Amber rolled Kim's window down, letting in the biting January air.

"I should have told someone," Kimberly said. Gasp of air. "What if this is my fault?" Gasp. "I should have ..." Gasp.

"Kim, honey, this *wasn't* your fault. None of it was your fault," Amber said, contemplating flooring the accelerator to get them to the coffee shop faster. Five more blocks. Two more minutes until the tonic wore off. "Inhale really slow and let it out. You're okay."

The cool air seemed to help a little, but Kimberly had a death grip on the door handle. Amber wasn't sure if Kim needed to hold onto something solid, or if she was planning to tuck, drop, and roll out of the car. The gasps soon morphed into long pulls of air into her nose and slow releases out her mouth.

"You were being a good friend by keeping it a secret," Amber said. "For upholding her wishes. She trusted you with something very important to her and you honored that. Her trust was in the right place."

Amber would have to process this information later. The reality that when it came to Melanie's deep, dark secret, she hadn't wanted Amber to know about it. Hadn't trusted her with it. Maybe if she had, Melanie would still be here.

It wasn't lost on Amber that she had been keeping a secret for even longer than Melanie had. Amber had never shared anything about her witch heritage with Melanie.

"Oh wow," Kimberly said, hand to her forehead. "I feel a little woozy—almost like a hangover." She held up her cup of hot chocolate and laughed softly. "What did you put in this thing?"

Yep, definitely needed less kava. It worked to calm people down, but also had the potential to make them feel a little high.

Then Kim placed a hand over her mouth, silencing another gasp. "I told you about Derrick! Oh crap. Oh crap, crap, crap. You won't tell, will you?" Sighing dramatically, she thunked her head against the headrest again. "The stress of everything is really getting to me."

"Of course I won't tell," Amber said, guilt coating her throat now; it pooled in her stomach. Her magic wasn't meant for this. It was meant for wonder and helping others. Not for turning someone like Kimberly into an even more high-strung mess than she already was. Not for unearthing secrets that were none of Amber's business.

But then Amber recalled the way Melanie had looked like a ghostly pale version of herself the last time Amber had seen her. The way Mel's hair had stuck her to face and neck with sweat. Her complaints about headaches. Her uncharacteristic fatigue.

Someone had *done* that to her.

Someone had poisoned her.

Had it been Whitney Sadler in a fit of jealousy?

If magic could lead Amber to her killer, why not use it? She wasn't a corrupt witch. She wasn't like the cursed Penhallows—a family of witches who only used their magic for personal gain. Amber knew her limits.

Pulling her car into the parking lot of the coffee shop, Amber shut off the vehicle and turned in her seat to look at Kimberly. The other woman had clearly been crying silently for the last minute or so.

Amber placed a hand on Kim's arm again; she flinched, clearly lost in her own thoughts. Her own tangled web of guilt. "You were a good friend."

Kim managed a small nod.

And I'm *going to be a good friend*, Amber thought, *and find out what Whitney Sadler actually knows. Maybe I can dump a little of the back-up vial of gossip tonic into everyone's coffee when they aren't looking.*

No.

No, she was a Blackwood, not a Penhallow.

But, if she *did* find out Whitney Sadler had anything to do with Melanie's death, Whitney would have one ticked-off witch to deal with.

CHAPTER 4

Purrcolate was part coffee shop, part co-op work space. It was by far the hippest establishment in Edgehill. Four years ago, there had been a considerable effort from the owners—and diehard patrons—of the well-established Clawsome Coffee, which had been around as long as Edgehill's cats, to keep Purrcolate from ever opening. But the two young Terrence brothers had won the town over once they'd explained their co-op work space idea.

Clawsome Coffee was done no favors by the owner, who was a hateful woman through and through. Before the Terrence brothers had come around, it hadn't mattered that Paulette was a monster, as she'd had a monopoly on the best coffee in town for years. One had to put up with her if you wanted the good stuff.

Purrcolate had been the first business to truly give Paulette a run for her money. And Paulette wasn't going down without a fight.

The space at Purrcolate was advertised to allow small businesses to have an affordable meeting place, give groups a safe space to congregate, and on Sunday afternoons, give students a quiet and free place to study. The Wi-Fi was promised to run at lightning speeds. Clawsome Coffee could only offer quality coffee and ambience; Paulette refused to modernize.

For the Here and Meow Committee, it gave the group of

five women and one stay-at-home dad a convenient place to discuss the festival twice a month for a nominal fee. Plus, Jack Terrence made amazing blueberry scones, and he always had a plate of them waiting, along with the complimentary coffee and tea they had for whoever booked the conference room.

Amber led the way through the shop now—offering a quick wave to Jack and Larry behind the counter as she went—and pushed open the mottled glass door to the conference room.

The room was plain. A large gray conference table took up most of the space, lined on both sides by comfortable black desk chairs. The table sat fourteen comfortably. The wall on the farthest end of the room had a large whiteboard fastened to it. The Here and Meow Committee used it during most meetings. A magnetized cup was attached to the board in the corner, with a colorful array of markers sprouting from it like a bouquet of flowers. Nothing else decorated the walls.

Ann Marie, Susie, Nathan, and Whitney were already inside. And had already plowed through half the scones.

Amber and Susie, as usual, avoided eye contact.

"Oh, Kim!" Ann Marie said, on her feet in an instant, hand to her chest. Ann Marie was almost a mirror image of Kim. They were both tall, thin brunettes. They both wore their hair long, but while Kim's was loose around her shoulders now, Ann Marie's was in a single braid down her back.

Amber glanced behind her, where Kimberly stood framed in the doorway, one bag over her shoulder, and the other two clutched tight in one hand. Her bottom lip shook.

"Oh my God, Ann Marie!"

Kimberly dropped her purses just inside the room, the door

44

swinging shut behind her as she hurried around one side of the table, while Ann Marie scurried the rest of the way to meet her. The two enveloped each other in a tight hug and immediately burst into tears.

Nathan, Susie, and Whitney's gazes shifted to their scones and coffee. When Ann Marie let out a choked cry, still clutching tight to Kimberly, Nathan's cheeks went pink. Embarrassed by the loud display of grief—or his lack of it—Amber couldn't be sure.

Amber grabbed Kimberly's discarded bags and dropped them into the open chair across from Nathan and Susie. When Amber pulled out the chair beside it for herself, she saw a white, ten-sided die resting by the table leg and surmised that the last group to use the room had been the Dungeons & Dragons meetup.

"How you holding up, Amber?"

She glanced across the table to see Whitney Sadler staring at her, her pretty little mouth pulled down in a slight frown. Her stick-straight blonde hair was pulled back into a high ponytail, accentuating her sharp cheekbones.

Amber shot a quick glance at Kim and Ann Marie, who still clutched each other tightly, their sobs shifting into muffled sniffling and whispers. Plopping into her chair, Amber sighed. "I keep hoping my phone will ring at any minute, I'll see her face pop up on the screen, and it'll all have been some kind of misunderstanding."

Susie scoffed, but tried to cover it up by taking a bite of scone. Amber ignored her.

Ann Marie let out another choked sob. "I miss her so much,"

she said, having extricated herself from Kimberly's grasp. She sniffed hard and swiped a finger under her nose. "I was supposed to meet her last week for dinner because she was starting to feel better, but I called it off because I just wanted to stay home for the night." She hiccuped, sniffing again. "That was my last chance to see her and I blew it off because I was being a lazy cow."

Kimberly pulled Ann Marie against her side again, hugging her. "Don't say such silly things! None of us could have known our time with her was going to be cut so short."

"She and I had a meeting planned on Monday, the day before," Whitney said. "I told her I would have to reschedule because I'd completely forgotten that Sydney's first fashion show meeting for the Here and Meow was happening. For the junior fashionista prodigies, you know?"

Amber did not know. And from the blank looks on everyone else's faces, no one else did, either. Whitney had a knack for making things about her and seemed flabbergasted when others weren't privy to the ins and outs of her schedule.

"Anyway," Whitney said, sniffing. "I was driving Sydney back to school in Belhaven that morning. To think I was having such a normal day and Melanie was …" She sighed. "If I had just made Derrick take Sydney to that fashion event instead, maybe meeting with Melanie would have … maybe she wouldn't be …"

The atmosphere in the room turned somber. Everyone struggled to make, let alone keep, eye contact.

"*You* were the last one to see her, weren't you, Amber?" a voice finally said, breaking the silence.

Amber's gaze shifted to the spot next to Nathan, where

46

Susie Paulson sat. Susie was the volunteer director and had been for as long as Whitney had been the finance chair. Over time, Susie had become brusque and to the point, her patience worn thin after dealing with a large portion of Edgehill's teenage population, who often signed up for the Here and Meow to gain volunteer credit for college applications. That was the common theory people had about Susie Paulson anyway, but Amber had known Susie for long enough to know the bad attitude had started much sooner.

Susie and Amber had worked together at the Paulsons' tea shop—Paws 4 Tea—after high school and hadn't gotten along well then. It had only gotten worse.

Kimberly cleared her throat, let go of Ann Marie, and made her way to sit beside Amber. "I don't know if I appreciate your tone, Susie," she said, moving her bags to the floor before sitting beside Amber.

"There was no tone," Susie said, not yet taking her eyes off Amber. "Was I mistaken, though? I heard Melanie had been in your shop just an hour or two before she … you know."

Ann Marie loudly blew her nose from the chair on Amber's other side.

All eyes turned to Amber then and she felt her face grow hot with some combination of anger and embarrassment, mostly because, now that the question was out there, Nathan, Ann Marie, and Whitney watched her expectantly. Like it was the question they'd all been wanting to ask, but didn't have Susie's same lack of tact.

"Yes," Amber said. "She came by because she had a

headache—*another* headache—and the meds she had weren't working. I gave her something to help her sleep."

"Yeah, sounds like it …" Susie muttered, face turned away as she pretended to find her scone terribly interesting again.

"*What* was that?" Amber said, leaning her arms on the table and angling a mildly concealed glare Susie's way. How she itched to put a spell on Susie's plate to turn it into a scuttling spider, to turn the legs of her chair to wiggly rubber, to turn the scone in her mouth to ash. "Is there something you need to say, *Susan*?"

Susie looked away from her scone then; she hated to be called Susan. "Guess we'll know if I have something to say when those results come back from Portland. Chief Brown sure seems to think we'll have a whole lot to talk about then."

Amber pursed her lips. "You really think I had something to do with this? You've known me for over fifteen years."

"And I know some seriously weird crap is sold in that store of yours," Susie said, tightly folding her arms across her chest. "Your teas and sweets and hot chocolate … they're all addicting. People swear by them. And others say there must be something … extra in your products to keep customers coming back."

Amber stared at her. "You think I'm *drugging* my customers? Are you upset because I actually *have*—"

"Ladies, c'mon," said Kimberly, cutting Amber off. "We're all stressed out. This is hard on all of us. We don't need to take it out on each other."

"I'm just stating for the record, that if we find out something … criminal happened to Melanie thanks to someone

48

in this room … that we rethink who's part of this committee," said Susie.

Amber was going to pluck this woman's eyes out. "You know what? I'm done here. I'm sorry, Kim." She stood abruptly. "I'll be back in an hour to take you home."

With that, she stormed out of the conference room, her magic like a physical thing writhing under her skin. High emotion always agitated her magic, like a caged lion circling its enclosure. It wanted out. It needed a release.

Heightened states also gave spells an extra kick.

Too bad she couldn't give an extra kick to Susie Paulson's face.

She stomped through the coffee shop, ignoring a shout of concern from Jack, and shoved her way out into the chilly evening. The brisk air hit her like a slap, cooling her skin and calming her magic. It was only by a fraction, but it might be enough to keep her from doing something stupid. Like deflating all of Susie's tires.

Halfway to her car, she heard someone shout her name.

If it was Susie, so help her.

Amber whirled around and Whitney Sadler came up short, her long ponytail swinging around to flop over one shoulder. Whitney held up her perfectly manicured hands, red lacquer shining under the lamplight, and slowly took several steps forward, as if approaching a wild animal.

Perhaps that wasn't far from the truth.

"I just wanted to make sure you were okay," Whitney said when they were a few feet apart. "Susie can be an ass when she's stressed out."

Amber wrinkled her nose at that.

"And she's usually stressed on days that end in a *y*," Whitney added.

With a laugh, Amber felt a little more of her magic settle. "I'm okay. Thanks for checking. I just … it's probably best if I sit these meetings out until …"

"None of the rest of us think you had anything to do with Mel," she said quickly. "Honestly. You loved Mel just as much as the rest of us, if not more. Susie is just being cruel because she's hurting, too, and she knew saying all that would get a rise out of you."

Amber sighed, knowing Whitney was likely right.

Talking to her now, a flare of guilt ignited in Amber's stomach. Amber was no better than Susie. Hadn't Amber hastily jumped to the conclusion that Whitney might have something to do with Melanie's death? It suddenly seemed as ludicrous a notion as Amber herself being responsible.

"Things will smooth out once nasty Owen Brown is forced to clear you of any involvement—at least as far as that vial is concerned," Whitney said.

Amber cocked a brow, as it very much sounded like Whitney assumed there was something else Owen could use against Amber.

"We both know he'll still suspect you even if there's no evidence to corroborate it."

Amber supposed the only consolation was that she hadn't been imagining Owen's dislike of her for all these years, and that it had been obvious to others too. Whitney smiled at her—a guarded, soft smile, but a smile nonetheless. It was clear she didn't want Amber to feel isolated. She wanted Amber to know that even though they'd never been close, she was on Amber's side.

Had Whitney even known Melanie and Derrick were having an affair? Maybe it would be just as shocking to Whitney as it had been to Amber.

"The real killer is still out there," Amber said. "I hate not knowing who could do something like this. I've lived here all my life and the idea of anyone in Edgehill being capable of it makes me sick to my stomach."

"I know what you mean," Whitney said, wrapping her arms around herself. Amber wasn't sure if it was due to the cold or something else.

"You …" Amber didn't know how to broach this subject. She was either going to put her foot in her mouth or open a can of worms. She didn't want to upset Whitney, especially not after she'd been kind enough to come check on her. "She told me that the mystery man she was seeing was from Marbleglen. Did she ever talk to you about him? Maybe he—"

"No. I don't know anything about him," Whitney said, dropping her arms to her sides. The friendly tone was gone, replaced now with something flat. "I mean, Mel never shut up about the guy—how kind and caring and what an 'attentive lover' he was. Went on and on like a lovesick teenager, but never told anyone his name. Never anything personal about him."

"Maybe he'll come forward to offer a lead," Amber said.

"I doubt it."

"Why—"

"I should get back," Whitney said. "If you decide you don't want to drive Kim home, I can take her."

Without waiting for a reply, Whitney turned on her heel, marched back to the coffee shop, and disappeared inside.

Amber parked behind the Quirky Whisker and slowly made her way around the side of the building, mulling over her conversation with Whitney. Though it was barely past 6:30, Russian Blue Avenue was quiet. Betty Harris was inside Purrfectly Scrumptious, lights blazing bright, but not a customer wandered her lobby. Not even Savannah the Maine Coon was out on the sidewalk, attempting to lure in patrons.

Cool air whipped across the parking lot, and Amber's senses tingled, her magic humming softly—a sure sign of rain.

Normally Amber stayed open until eight on Fridays, but she'd put a note on her magicked blackboard to let visitors know she would be closed early that night due to Here and Meow duties.

When she rounded the corner of her modest brick building, she didn't expect to find anyone loitering outside. And yet, a man in a black peacoat, hands cupped around his eyes as he peered through the glass into the dark interior of the shop, was doing just that.

"The sign says we're closed until tomorrow," she said when she was a few feet away.

The man gave a start and whirled to face her.

Recognition hit her instantly, quickly followed by an

involuntary groan of annoyance. It was Connor Declan from the *Edgehill Gazette*. She really didn't want to deal with a nosy reporter right now. She also wasn't sure what it meant for her if he was here. Had he been tipped off by Chief Brown that something "interesting" had been discovered by the crime lab in Portland?

Not that there could possibly be anything interesting *to* find. Unless someone was trying to set her up. Which couldn't be the case. She wasn't in a crime novel. This was Edgehill, where the only truly interesting thing about it—having a practicing witch—was a secret.

Besides, Owen Brown couldn't find her quirks so distasteful that he'd try to frame her, right?

Connor recovered quickly and shoved his hands into the pockets of his coat, the collar of which was pulled up to shield his neck from the chilly night air. The tip of his nose was a little pink. How long had he been waiting out here?

"I'm more interested in you than in the shop," he said.

Amber's brows arched toward her hairline.

"Oh. Crap. That sounded more provocative than I meant it," he said, his cheeks flushing a bit to match the hue of his nose. "I just wanted to start a dialogue with you about a story I'm writing." He must have gathered from her expression that she was not in the mood for this, because he stumbled over his next words. "About … about Melanie Cole."

Amber could only imagine what he wanted to have a "dialogue" about. *Edgehill's Own Freak Poisons the Town's Newest and Most Beloved Resident!* the headline might say. *But why, you ask? Read on to find out!*

Maybe he should be having a "dialogue" with Susie Paulson. Amber was sure Susie could provide Connor with all kinds of theories about why Amber would have it out for Melanie.

Amber moved past him to unlock her door, and though he sidled out of the way, he didn't make any attempt to leave. Once the latch disengaged, she glanced over her shoulder at him. "I'm not interested."

He slunk into the shop after her with all the grace of a cat. "Just a few minutes, I promise. I heard it from the grapevine that the results from the test in Portland came back and nothing remotely sinister was found in that vial Melanie purchased from here."

Chief Brown must have friends in high places to get the results back so quickly.

Unable to help herself, she turned to him, eyes wide. "Do they have any idea what happened to her then? How she was poisoned?"

The shop door shut, filling the quiet space with the tinkle of bells. The only light in the store came from the streetlights lining the sidewalk and the glow from Purrfectly Scrumptious across the street. Out of the corner of her eye, she could see Betty Harris hovering in her doorway, watching.

Connor cocked his head at Amber. "How do you know she was poisoned? That's something I found out about only today. I know rumors were going around about foul play, but her specifically being poisoned wasn't confirmed until a couple hours ago. And certainly not to the general public."

Well, she couldn't very well tell him she'd gotten a flash of blue lips and nails thanks to a thought-reveal spell she'd conducted on the chief of police. "Kimberly Jones was the one who found her. She mentioned that Melanie's lips looked almost blue, and I happen to know a lot about herbs." She motioned vaguely at her shop. "What she described sounded like a poisoning to me. It was an educated guess."

Connor narrowed his eyes slightly, as if he thought if he changed his perspective of her face, he could better ascertain whether she was lying.

Great, someone else who questioned her moral character.

"If I've been cleared of suspicion—more or less—what do you want to talk to me about?" she asked, hoping to redirect his attention.

"It wouldn't be an official interview, just a chat," he said, the creases in his brow smoothing out.

Amber wasn't a fan of cryptic answers, but she had a feeling she would have a hard time getting rid of the guy if she didn't at least indulge him a little. Plus, wouldn't outright refusal make her look even more suspicious?

"Fine," she said, turning back to the door to flip the lock. She offered the still-watching Betty a wave.

Betty frowned, then returned the gesture. She disappeared back into her own shop.

Amber flipped on the lights, then walked past Connor, slipping out of her jacket as she did. She rounded the side of the long counter that stretched across one end of the store, draping her coat over a high-backed stool she used to reach the higher shelves lined with jars and tinctures and baskets of dried herbs. She dropped her purse onto the worn leather seat.

Turning around, she found him standing on the other

side of the counter, gaze roaming the labeled drawers just behind her. Connor had lived in Edgehill as long as she had, yet this was the first time she could remember him being inside the Quirky Whisker. They had spoken a handful of times—pleasant hellos and how are yous—but nothing that would truly constitute a conversation.

When it came to Here and Meow coverage in the *Edgehill Gazette*, Connor's stories and Amber's strange animated toys had yet to cross paths.

If Amber remembered correctly, in high school Willow had a raging crush on Connor Declan. He'd been more of an artsy kid in school—wearing all black and doing mic night poetry readings at a dive bar on the edge of town. Willow had been part of that scene back then, especially after their parents died.

While Willow had funneled her grief deeper into her artistic side, Amber had retreated into herself, lost in not just her grief, but her guilt. She'd been too closed off then to develop out-of-control crushes on boys like Connor.

"Hello?" he said now, waving a hand in front of Amber.

"I … sorry," Amber said, giving her head a light shake. "It's been a long night." Resting her hands on the counter, she scanned his face. It was quite a nice face, really. The clean-shaven, short-cropped hair look suited him far better than the shaggy 'do and guy-liner from high school. "Ready when you are."

He slipped a hand into his pocket.

"Is this on the record or off?" she asked.

His hand stilled. Slowly, he removed it, empty. Amber

thought she caught sight of a notepad's white corner sticking out of his pocket. "Off." Resting a hip against the counter, he folded his arms. "Just a chat."

"Shoot," she said.

"What do you know about Melanie's life before she moved to Edgehill?" Connor asked. "Anything about her old job?"

She'd expected him to mention the secret Derrick Sadler relationship as a means to throw her off. She had to assume Melanie's affair was a well-known secret at this point, but it was Amber who was thrown now. Melanie had talked about her old job even less than she'd discussed her mystery man. "Just that she worked at a marketing firm in California that focused on getting new products off the ground."

Connor nodded. "Did she talk to you about why she left the firm?"

Amber's brow furrowed. Did he know the answer and was testing her knowledge of her friend's past, or was he fishing for information himself?

The more questions people asked about Melanie, the more she realized she might not have known the woman as well as she thought. They'd gone out to dinner and hung out and watched movies and planned for the Here and Meow. But Amber hadn't pried into Melanie's past—except for the ever-lingering mystery of who she'd been dating—anymore than Melanie had pried into Amber's.

Had Melanie enjoyed Amber's friendship *because* she'd never harassed her about her past?

A knot of frustration formed in Amber's gut.

Mentally muttering the same thought-reveal spell she'd

used on the chief, Amber reached out to put a hand on Connor's arm, who still wore his peacoat. "Do you think her death was connected to her old job somehow?"

Just as with the chief, the lack of skin-on-skin contact wouldn't allow her to get a true thought. Instead, she'd see a snapshot of memory pulled up by the question she'd asked.

A flash of a building's façade popped into her head, the words "Northwind Consultants" printed in blocky white letters above a set of double glass doors. Melanie, several years younger, if her bob haircut was any indication, reached for one of the handles. Another flash—this time of a younger Derrick Sadler, smiling at something Amber couldn't see.

Amber quickly pulled her hand away, trying to disguise the movement by running said hand through her loose hair. "Would you like tea or anything?"

Connor offered her another "what are you up to, Amber Blackwood?" squinty-eyed look. Amber truly wondered if he'd been a cat in a past life. Only cats could judge you so effectively with just a subtle glance. Then his gaze flicked over her shoulder to the wall of shelves and drawers. His nose crinkled a fraction. "I'm fine, thanks."

Unlike the thought-images she'd received from Owen Brown—a flash of memory he'd actually seen—the ones she'd gotten from Connor felt different. These were pieced together. Like the collages she'd made in high school from cut-up magazines. They weren't direct images from his bank of memories; they were crafted by his mind, based on gathered information.

It was enough to give Amber insight. And she hoped what

she said next wouldn't unveil Melanie's secrets, but rather confirm Connor's suspicions.

"I know she had a connection to Edgehill before she ever moved here, since she knew Derrick Sadler through her work at Northwind," Amber said. "She didn't talk much about her time there, just that there'd been a falling out."

This last part was pure speculation. Whitney and Derrick had been together for at least twelve years, given their twelve-year-old daughter Sydney. If Melanie's overall appearance told Amber anything, it was that she didn't think it was possible Melanie had met Derrick *before* Whitney had been in the picture. But how long had Melanie's secret relationship with Derrick been going on? Certainly longer than six months.

Amber tried to recall her conversation with Whitney earlier, how her demeanor had changed when Amber had mentioned Melanie's "mystery man." How much did Whitney know about Melanie's seemingly long-lasting entanglement with her husband?

And what was Derrick's connection to Northwind Consultants? The Sadlers had lived in Edgehill for their entire marriage, and a few years before that. Amber realized she wasn't sure she knew what Derrick Sadler did for a living.

"Falling out is putting it lightly," Connor said.

When Amber's brow furrowed, he didn't elaborate. Amber filed that away for something she'd need to look into later.

Connor switched track then and asked how Melanie and Amber had become friends.

"Through the Here and Meow festival. Melanie visited my booth and was so enamored with my animated toys that she bought a pig and a horse. Melanie didn't live in Edgehill then, but she told me that day that she fell so in love with the town, she wished she could live here. A week later, she quit her job in California, packed up her things, and drove to Edgehill."

Amber had always adored this town, so it hadn't struck her as remotely strange that someone would give up everything to move here. But now she wondered if the abrupt way Melanie had uprooted her life should have been a red flag.

Melanie had seemed to love her decision, folding herself into Edgehill with ease as if she'd always lived here. And after only a year, she'd been voted in as the head of the cat festival. A vote that was as much about a person's skill and reliability, as it was a popularity contest.

The town had overwhelmingly voted her in. Chosen her. Accepted her as one of its own.

"Do you think anyone on the committee was jealous that she was voted into the top leadership position so quickly?" Connor asked.

On the one hand, Amber thought it was ridiculous anyone would want to head a committee of *anything* so desperately that they'd kill over it, but then she remembered the bloody bar brawl that had been started over a lot less.

When Amber didn't say anything, Connor continued. "The person who could most obviously benefit from Melanie's death would be Kimberly Jones," he said. "Melanie's death left the seat vacant and Kimberly thereby got the coveted position."

Amber had started shaking her head before Connor had even finished the statement. "You didn't see … didn't hear her—" Taking a calming breath, she said, "You didn't hear her after she found Melanie. She could barely talk. The slightest mention of Melanie still sets her off."

Connor shrugged. "I've seen this kind of thing before. She could be a great actress. That, or the shame of what she's done out of greed is so overwhelming to her now that she has intense bouts of emotion because she regrets her actions."

Amber had known Kimberly for most of her life. She'd always been the type of person to react emotionally, whether it was directly about her or not. And she'd also seen Kimberly try out for a school play once, and ... well, acting wasn't a skill set she would claim Kim had.

"Who got Kimberly's position as assistant festival director once Kim became director?" Connor asked.

"No one," Amber said. "Not yet, anyway. I was just telling Kim today that she might need one. But if the details of that were discussed in tonight's meeting, I missed it."

"Oh?" he asked.

"I had a bit of a ... confrontation with Susie Paulson and bailed on the meeting before it had a chance to start."

Connor's lip curled at the mention of Susie's name. "Miss Paulson is in the same camp as Chief Owen when it comes to theories about your involvement, I gather?"

"You could say that," Amber said.

"Any reason why she might think you'd want to hurt Melanie?" he asked.

At least he wasn't looking at her the way the others had in the meeting. That look of barely contained suspicion. He was merely curious.

"Oh, I don't know," said Amber. "Susie and I have just

never gotten along. She works at the tea shop on Himalayan Way, you know?"

Connor nodded.

"Well, her family has owned the place for ages," Amber said. "I opened up here about five years ago, after working at Paws 4 Tea for a while after high school, and a lot of the customers from there followed me here. The Paulsons, Susie especially, have never quite forgiven me. She even accused me of drugging customers to lure them in." Amber fought an eye roll. Sometimes it felt like they'd never actually graduated high school.

"She called the newspaper recently, demanding to talk to a reporter," Connor said, then paused, as if debating his next words, not sure how much he should tell her. "I had just come back from a lunchbreak, and I didn't know she'd already called in the two days before. So my lovely co-workers pawned her off on me. Let me tell you, that woman is *very* upset you've stolen her business."

"Stolen is a bit extreme," Amber said.

It wasn't lost on Amber that Connor had *known* Susie and Amber had a sketchy past, yet had questioned her as if he hadn't.

"She also accused you of price gouging and bribery."

"Oh, please!" said Amber. "It's not my fault the Paulsons mostly buy store-bought teas and repackage them and pretend they're homemade. My tea actually *is*."

"Touchy," he said, smiling now.

She fought her own smile. "Maybe."

Granted, Amber also had her magic to help her produce

and package her teas far quicker than the Paulson foursome combined. Susie inherently knew that, but she couldn't figure out Amber's secret. So now Susie just accused her of whatever she could think of, hoping she eventually landed on something that resembled the truth.

Now it had morphed into veiled accusations of murder. It was truly ridiculous.

"Anyone else who might have it out for you or Melanie?"

"*Me?*" Amber asked.

"Either it was a coincidence that she collapsed with that vial in her hand, or whoever poisoned her made sure it was there in order to shift suspicion onto you—no matter how temporary."

Amber sighed, suddenly exhausted. "No, I can't think of anyone. Especially no one on the committee. Everyone loved Mel. She—"

A soft series of bells sounded then—a distant sound, though clearly coming from inside the shop—and Amber gave a start. It was her cell phone. It rang so rarely that a trill of panic went through her whenever she heard it. Especially since it should have been in her coat pocket where she last left it—at least she thought so. Goodness knew where the thing was now. And she couldn't use a locator spell with Connor here.

The sound stopped, and Amber held her breath, waiting for the tinkling to start up again. When it did, she darted around the side of the counter and hurried toward the sound—somewhere near the toy display, she thought. The sound stopped and so did she, waiting. "Crap. I can never remember where I left the thing."

Connor came up beside her. "Does this happen often?"

"Only every other day."

The ringing started up. "Oh!" And she was off again, hurrying around the pyramid-shaped toy shelf, topped with Scarlet the red dragon.

Ahead of her was a wall of empty mason jars of all sizes. Hung from various places on the shelf's face were clutches of dried lavender and sage. Connor was beside her, head cocked like a dog.

Amber spotted the telltale blue glow of her phone's screen just moments before Connor reached forward and plucked it from underneath a small stack of journals on the ground. Willow's smiling face appeared on the screen for a brief moment, then vanished as the call went to voicemail.

"How *is* Willow?" he asked as he handed her the phone.

"She's good," said Amber, slipping the phone into her back pocket. "Moving and shaking in Portland still."

"She wasn't made for this place," he said.

Amber couldn't tell if that was a compliment or not. "Why haven't you left?"

"Well, I did for a while. I went to college out of state."

"Ah, that's right. University of Michigan, right?" she said. "So, I guess the better question is: why did you come back? Willow left and stayed gone."

"She comes home for the Here and Meow, doesn't she?"

"Sure, but visiting a few times a year isn't the same as putting down roots."

He considered that for a moment. "Why do *you* stay?"

Connor never seemed to answer a direct question with a direct answer.

"It's home. I've never known anything else," she said. "Something keeps me here."

He paused for a long time, staring at the ground. The tips of his ears went pink this time—from embarrassment, not the cold. "Is it because of your parents?"

There wasn't anyone in Edgehill—either residents who'd lived here then, or people who'd moved here after—who didn't know about the house fire that had killed the Blackwood parents. A select few, Amber included, thought there was something strange about the fire. Amber had heard from neighbors that the fire had turned into a blazing inferno faster than should have been possible. That the flames had burned blue.

The only family member related to the Blackwoods who remained in Edgehill now, aside from herself, was a cousin. The man was in his mid-to-late thirties and "off his nut," according to Aunt Gretchen. But at the time, he'd told anyone who would listen that he'd sensed they were in danger that night and had rushed over to save them. He said they hadn't burned peacefully in their beds while they slept, but that they'd been trapped inside the house, unable to get out.

Later that month, her cousin Edgar had been checked into a mental hospital in Belhaven. When police had come to question him, he'd recanted his story. Said he hadn't been anywhere near the house on Ocicat Lane at the time of the fire and had no idea why he'd claimed that he had.

Some little part of Amber still wondered if it had been true. Edgar was a shut-in now. He wouldn't take her calls or open the door when she came knocking. So a few years ago, she'd given up.

"Maybe," she said now. "I know it sounds silly, but I'm kind of all they have left in Edgehill. I know they're dead and gone, but … if they're out there watching somehow, I want them to know I'm still here."

Her cheeks flushed. She had no idea why she'd said any of that. Emotions had run too high today. That was it. She needed to take a hot shower, find a good book, curl up with Alley and Tom, and just forget about everything for a while.

Divulging personal, well, anything, to virtual strangers was not her modus operandi.

"I don't think that's silly at all," he said. "In my family—"

Amber flinched when her back pocket started to ring. She did her best to ignore it. Had Connor been about to divulge his *own* personal information? She could call Willow later.

Without looking, she pulled out her phone long enough to send the call to voicemail.

Mere moments later, the ringing resumed.

Not now, Willow!

"You going to answer that?" Connor asked, eyebrows raised. "Seems important …"

Amber looked at the screen to see that it wasn't Willow calling, but Kimberly. Crap! She had been supposed to pick her up after the meeting. "I should probably …"

"Of course," he said. "I should be going anyway. Would it be okay to come talk to you again about Melanie?"

"Sure," Amber said, not sure what else there would be

to discuss. Connor seemed to know more about her than Amber did.

Amber unlocked the door for him, the door's bells tinkling. Rain had started to fall, blowing in sideways sheets thanks to the steady wind.

"Have a nice night, Amber," Connor said, adjusting his collar to work as a windscreen. "We'll speak again ... very soon."

As Amber closed and locked the door behind him, watching him hurry down the wet sidewalk, she wondered why that had sounded like a threat.

CHAPTER 5

Most of the car ride with Kimberly on their way back from Purrcolate was awkward at best. The rain came down in thick sheets, the windshield wipers working double time. Kimberly tried in vain to convince Amber no one truly thought she was a murderer.

When Kim finally realized Amber wasn't replying, merely white-knuckling the steering wheel as she headed for Kim's house, she switched topics.

"Whitney and Susie were acting *real* chummy in the parking lot while I was waiting for you."

"Really?" Amber asked, shooting her a glance, unable to help herself.

Kimberly sat a little straighter, clearly pleased that she'd finally said something to pull Amber out of her brooding.

"Yep! The meeting went along like usual, but instead of people going off their separate ways afterwards, those two were in a really animated conversation by Susie's car. I swear those two hardly ever talk to each other. I'm not saying Whitney is stuck up, exactly, but she's always had a certain type of friend, you know? And we're all *not* it."

Kimberly wasn't wrong.

"No idea what they were talking about?" Amber asked.

"Not a clue," Kim said. "I was trying to ignore them, mostly because I can't believe Susie was talking to you like that. Whitney threw her hands in the air, like she was really frustrated with something Susie said, and then Whitney stomped off. Susie got in her car and practically burned rubber to get away. Whitney came over to ask if I needed a ride, but I said I was waiting for you. I swear, she made a face like she smelled something bad, and then she left without saying anything else." She paused for a breath. "I'm really glad you called back. I was all alone by then."

Amber winced. "Sorry, I would have been there sooner, but Connor Declan showed up."

"Oh really?" Kimberly asked, and Amber didn't need to look at her to know she was waggling her eyebrows suggestively. "Business or pleasure? That man is a tall, *tall* drink of water."

Yep, they were definitely still in high school.

"Business," Amber said. "He wanted to talk about Melanie."

"Oh," Kimberly said, voice soft. "Has there been any news about … you know? Is that why he came to talk to you?"

Amber chewed on her bottom lip. She didn't for a second think Kim had poisoned Melanie, despite Connor's argument that Kim would have benefitted the most from Melanie's death. Should she tell Kim what Connor had said about what killed her? The news would be circulating soon enough. "He found out she was poisoned."

Kimberly let out a choked sob, fingers pressed to her lips for a moment. "Oh, poor Mel."

"I know," Amber said. "I just hope it wasn't horribly painful."

"She looked like she was sleeping, for what it's worth," Kim muttered, gaze focused on her lap. She worried at a piece of skin near her cuticle.

The car ride was quiet after that.

Amber and Kim exchanged an awkward in-the-car hug before Kim piled out with all her bags, offered a quick wave, and wandered up to her house with a slow, shuffling walk.

That wasn't the way a killer acted, was it?

No, Kim was just as upset about all this as Amber.

She drove home with nothing but the sound of rain pattering her windshield for company.

Though Kim had assured Amber that no one other than Susie thought Amber was the culprit, Amber grew more desperate to solve the mystery of Melanie's death, if only so people would stop thinking she'd had anything to do with it. It wasn't like the officer leading the investigation had her best interest at heart.

After climbing the steps to her studio apartment, Amber dropped her things to the floor by the top of the stairs and draped her wet raincoat over the back of a chair. Then she walked to her bed, flopped onto her back, and let out a huffing sigh. Alley issued a cry of protest over having her sleep disrupted and jumped from the bed to the window bench seat in a graceful leap. Tom draped himself over Amber's stomach, limbs spread out on either side of her body. His rumbling purr started up moments later.

Amber liked to think Tom was attuned to her feelings and sensed she needed comfort, but she knew the reality was that he just liked to sleep on anything warm. Plus, rain made him anxious. She let his purr relax her.

She replayed the conversation with Kim, and then the one with Connor. The images he'd unknowingly shared flitted through her mind. A younger Melanie working at Northwind Consultants. The implication that, while working there, she'd met Derrick Sadler. Derrick Sadler who more than likely had already been very married by then.

Why had Whitney been chastising Susie in the parking lot?

Amber lay there like a distraught starfish for a while, letting Tom soak up her warmth.

Minutes, maybe hours, later, a burst of sound startled Amber out of her near-slumber. Tom jumped when she did, hissing just in case the thing that had woken him was a physical assailant. Just as quickly, in true attack-cat fashion, he darted off the bed and underneath it.

Amber hurried to her purse, still sitting on the floor next to the top of the stairs, and plucked out her phone. Willow smiled up at her. Amber had completely forgotten to call her back. She hit accept.

"Hello, dear sister," Willow said in greeting. "How nice of you to finally take my call."

Amber wrinkled her nose.

Dropping the false mocking tone, Willow said, "How you holding up?"

"Best as I can be, I suppose," she said. "Why are you calling *me* on a Friday night, by the way? And twice, at that."

"Stayed in."

"Who are you and what have you done with my sister?"

Willow's laugh was high and light and never failed to make Amber smile. "I actually have to go into the office tomorrow. Our new client is being super fussy. His restaurant opens in two weeks and he just decided he hates *all* his promotional materials—he loved them yesterday—so I have to go in super early for a rush job tweaking his logo. Again."

Amber's mother had always told her that their magic linked them together as a family. That when one Blackwood needed something, their shared magic would call out, like a distress beacon. Had her magic reached out to Willow's, prompting her little sister to call her? Willow always seemed to know when Amber was in need, and vice versa; Amber often wondered if it was a sisterly bond or something more.

The thought-reveal spell Amber had used on Connor had shown her that Melanie used to work at a company that specialized in getting new businesses off the ground. It wasn't unlike what Willow did for clients, though Willow's company only dealt with the design side of things.

"Hey, super weird question," Amber said.

"My favorite kind!"

"Have you heard of Northwind Consultants?"

"Yeah, of course."

Amber cocked an eyebrow her sister couldn't see. "Not 'of course.' How do you know about them?"

Willow paused for long enough that Amber knew she, too, had raised an eyebrow her sister couldn't see. "Why? You finally thinking of going bigtime like I've been telling you since, oh, forever, and selling your animated toys on a larger scale?"

"No, nothing like that."

Amber caught her sister up on everything that had happened since the day Melanie died, until tonight's meeting that Amber had run out on. She got worked up during her retelling and paced her small studio. Tom eyed her warily.

"I'm going to wring that Susie Paulson's neck!" Willow said. "Her brother was in the same class as me and he was just as petty as Susie."

Amber could always count on Willow to be on her side. "Then none other than Connor Declan came by to talk to me."

"You're kidding!"

Amber walked over to her window and gazed out at Edgehill. At her old house in the distance. "He asked how you were."

"Be still my heart," she said. "I had it so bad for that guy in high school."

"He's a total straight-laced journalist now," Amber said, sitting on the window seat, back to the town. She absently scratched Alley behind the ears. "He's the one who I got the name Northwind Consultants from."

"Another thought-reveal spell?"

"Yep," Amber said. "What do they do at Northwind?"

"Well, they work exclusively with new businesses. They work with tech companies more than most, I think, but they'll work with up-and-coming restaurants a lot—especially if they're part of some new trend. Like cronuts or rolled ice cream. They're *the* company for that in California. Their clientele usually has lots of money to spend, so they go all out on creative marketing. We've actually worked with them a couple of times when they needed some design work for a dessert place that opened in Portland. The owner is one of those fancy bakers from the Food Network."

"Guess that explains why Mel was such a whiz at marketing," Amber said. "She had all these ideas cooking for the Here and Meow that no one had ever even thought of before."

"Sounds about right," Willow said. "They only hire the best of the best over there."

Amber mulled that over. "I just can't figure out what the connection is to Derrick Sadler."

"Yeah. I have no idea what the Sadlers do," Willow said. "I just remember them having a lot of money. I can ask around at the office later. A bunch of us have to go in to work on this dang restaurant job."

Amber stood up again. Walked to her bed. Sat down. She felt restless. "Cool. Yeah. That would be great."

Willow sighed. "Are you sure you're okay? You sound exhausted."

"I'm okay," Amber said, rubbing a hand back and forth across her eyes. "When are you coming to see me?"

"I need to be here until the launch of this restaurant, then you and I can work on Here and Meow stuff for as long as you need. I have a week of vacation time blocked off and I can work remotely if something at the office blows up."

"Damn you and your success," Amber said.

Willow laughed. Amber smiled to herself.

"Well, I should head to bed," Willow said, muffling a yawn. "I just wanted to check in."

"Thanks, Will."

After hanging up, Amber scanned her little studio. Tom

was now curled up with Alley on the window seat. There was no way she'd be able to sleep anytime soon, so she sat in front of her laptop at her dining room table and booted it up.

If Willow's magic *had* called out to her own, then Amber shouldn't ignore it.

She searched Northwind Consultants first, finding a sleek website that didn't offer much more than what Willow had already told her. She searched the page of current employees and wasn't surprised to see that Derrick Sadler wasn't listed.

Next, she searched for Derrick himself. He was a handsome man in his mid-forties. His dark hair had started to gray at the temples, but that only made him all the more appealing. It was clear the man spent a decent amount of time in the gym, and he had an easy smile.

He had several social media pages, all focused mostly on his accounting business, with occasional pictures of his wife, cats, and on rare occasions, their daughter Sydney. Did Derrick work as a private accountant for Northwind Consultants? If Willow was right, and the majority of Northwind's clientele was well-to-do, having a gig as their accountant could likely earn him a pretty penny.

Amber scoured his pages for any direct mention of Northwind Consultants but didn't find it. She did find a contact page on Derrick's site for Sadler Accounting though, along with the promise of a free quote.

She penned him a quick message before she could talk herself out of it.

Dear Mr. Sadler,

I would like to take you up on the free quote offer. With

the growth of my business at the Quirky Whisker, I fear I'm getting to the point where I need to work with an accountant. Plus, I'm thinking of expanding the business in the next year or two and will need some financial advice on how to go about that.

Please let me know when your next available appointment is.

Best,

Amber Blackwood

She quickly hit send.

Derrick's online presence revealed little else. Not a single "I was having an affair with a woman who was recently found dead" tell-all blog post anywhere. Rude.

Whitney Sadler's media presence was more personal—pictures of her and her pretty girlfriends at brunch, drinking mimosas; playing tennis in a crisp white skirt; lying out by the pool in a black bikini with a fruity drink adorned with a tiny umbrella, the glass sweating on a spotless side table. Her life looked like a series of magazine ads.

Kimberly had accurately assessed that Amber and the rest of the Here and Meow Committee—most of Edgehill, really—weren't in the Sadlers' league. Amber often wondered why they lived here, of all places, and not some jet-setting city like Los Angeles or New York City.

And then Amber saw the smiling face of the Sadlers' twelve-year-old daughter. Sydney, from what Amber could find, went to a boarding school in the nearby town of Belhaven, about an hour outside Edgehill. In one of the few pictures of the girl, she wore a school uniform with the distinctive eagle logo for Waterton Prep, a place nestled in the mountains.

Had Derrick truly been planning to leave Whitney for Melanie? Even when they had a child in the picture?

Another hour of snooping yielded little else. Amber's magic was useless to her when she had no idea what to do next. Any spells about a specific person were unavailable to her without a personal item from the person in question. Or, at the very least, a picture to look at. Even still, without knowing what to search for, her magic would flounder. It wasn't worth the spent energy.

Amber slapped her laptop shut and got ready for bed. She gave the cats their late-night snack and plugged in her cell phone, as the rarely-used device had issued a warning beep that the battery now hovered just below five percent.

With the lights off, Amber laid awake, Alley curled up at the foot of the bed, and Tom snoozing on a pillow by Amber's head. Moonlight poured in through the window, the curtains still open. Even while lying down, she could make out the shape of her unfinished family home out in the distance.

Her phone trilled.

With her heart racing, she rolled over and hung off the side of her bed so she could check her messages while the phone stayed plugged into the wall.

Derrick Sadler had replied to her message.

Hello, Amber!

I would be happy to meet with you to discuss the financial future of the Quirky Whisker. My daughter will be delighted to know I am talking to the infamous Amber

Blackwood, creator of her favorite toys. We get one for her every year for her birthday. The waddling duck is still her favorite.

I'm booked through most of next week, but I have a noon slot open on Wednesday. If that works for you, please drop by the office and we can have a chat.

Best,

Derrick

P.S. I was terribly sorry to hear about the loss of your friend Melanie Cole. She seemed like a wonderful woman.

Amber shook her head. At least she knew she could go into the meeting with Derrick with the knowledge that he had no problem lying. Melanie *seemed* like a wonderful woman?

Oh, Derrick. You can do better than that.

She was glad he'd replied so quickly, at least. Though she wondered if the late-hour response had more to do with the postscript than it did with his enthusiasm for the job.

Now she had to figure out the best way to pump the guy for information.

Since Amber didn't know Derrick, she didn't think it wise to rely on a tonic she could slip into his drink. What if he had nothing during the meeting to slip said tonic into? No, she would need to get a charmed item into his hands. Something she could hand him that would trigger her spell of choice once his skin touched the object in question.

A business card seemed most likely, but it wasn't as if he didn't already know who she was. What use would a business card be to him? What if he saw it and waved it off, claiming he didn't need it?

Her gaze drifted to her coffee table, which sat piled high with books and plastic pieces and sheets of paper covered in half-formed spells. And then it clicked.

She would make Sydney Sadler a new toy. The girl had been partial to the duck, so Amber would craft her another bird. Perhaps the peacock—the one she'd been working on for months. The act of flipping up its tail and fanning it out had never quite worked. The last attempt had resulted in the tail snapping off altogether.

Flinging back her comforter, Amber climbed out of bed and turned on the lights.

She had a lot of work to do before Wednesday.

CHAPTER 6

While fast at work behind her counter on Saturday afternoon, Amber was startled out of her concentration when the chime above her door sounded. Weekends were often a little busier at the Quirky Whisker during the winter, but it was still a bit of a shock when someone came in during the slow months.

When her gaze landed on the seemingly lost woman, Amber popped off her stool so quickly, it clattered to the ground. The woman flinched, then locked eyes with Amber. Amber's tiny paintbrush dropped out of her hand and onto the counter, rolling away from her and leaving a trail of tiny purple splotches as it went. Muttering a curse, she placed the plastic tail feather she'd been painting down on the counter next to the already painted blue-and-green ones. She hoped the paint wouldn't stain the wood.

"Are you Amber Blackwood?" the woman asked, taking a few tentative steps into the shop. The door closed behind her, sending the bell above it into a snit once more.

The woman was the spitting image of Melanie. Amber blinked, shook her head, then looked again. She was the spitting image of what Melanie *would* have looked like in twenty years. Same build, same long brown hair, same pretty features.

This woman's face had started to age, but expertly applied makeup kept her looking younger than her years.

"Uh … yes," Amber said. "Sorry. I … you look just like her." She hurried around the counter, wiping her hands on her apron as she did, hoping any paint that had gotten onto her fingers was dry by now. She held out a hand.

The woman's bottom lip shook and then she pulled Amber into a tight hug. Amber hugged her back, letting the woman cry on her shoulder for a minute.

Pulling back, the woman apologized and frantically searched through her purse, still sniffling. "I'm so sorry," she said, as she pulled out a tissue packet. "I just … she talked about you all the time. You were her closest friend here, you know? I know how fiercely private Mel could be, so it … it says a lot that she was so fond of you."

Amber frowned. "I was quite fond of her too."

They stood in awkward silence for a while as Melanie's mother got herself under control.

"Oh God, where are my manners?" she asked, wiping her eyes and sniffing loudly once before shaking out her hands like she was preparing for a boxing match. "I'm Nicolette Cole. I'm here … I came to Edgehill both to identify her body and to give consent for an autopsy. That all needs to happen before I can plan … the funeral."

"*Oh.*"

"I can't believe this is happening …" Nicolette broke into sobs again.

Amber wrapped an arm around Nicolette's shoulders and ushered her behind the counter. She righted the stool and gently eased Nicolette onto it. As the woman continued to cry, face buried in her hands, Amber scrambled to make a mug of her famous hot chocolate.

Toward the back of the shop—near the door that led up to her second-floor studio apartment—was a little cooking station. The small nook had a sink on one side and enough counter space on the other for a hot plate. A three-rack shelf hung above the sink and contained all manner of teas, cocoa, sugars, and various spices—like Kimberly's beloved cayenne pepper. Two rows of white mugs, emblazoned with the Quirky Whisker logo, hung beneath the shelf on hooks.

Amber took down a mug, heated a kettle, and peered around the little wall of her cooking alcove to check on Nicolette. The poor woman still wept.

Once the cocoa was finished, Amber crept behind the counter. Since Nicolette wasn't paying her any mind, Amber was able to rummage through her collection of ready-made tinctures without raising suspicion. She scanned the white cards on the faces of the drawers until she found one for "calming the troubled mind." There were three vials here, one containing a more potent mixture than the other two. She hesitated for a moment. Her tinctures had always been a little … unreliable. But this was one she'd tested on Willow the last time she'd been home. The worst that could happen would be Nicolette feeling a bit drunk. When emotions were high, calming tinctures worked to swing said emotions back into a more neutral zone.

Grabbing the strongest of the three, Amber waved a hand

over the vial while muttering the quick activation spell and then poured the clear liquid into the steaming hot chocolate.

Amber rounded the counter to stand on the customer side and set the mug down in front of Nicolette with a soft thud. The woman started and looked up. When she didn't move, Amber pushed the mug a little closer. "Drink this. You'll feel better," she said. "It's one of my specialties."

Nicolette's face was red and splotchy from crying. With a wadded-up tissue still clutched in her fist, she reached forward, cupping the mug with both hands. "It smells really good."

Amber frowned at how small the woman's voice was. So broken.

Nicolette took a sip. Swallowed. Took another.

After several long moments, Nicolette's shoulders relaxed. The deep lines between her brows smoothed out. Then she let out a soft sigh.

"This stuff is amazing!" She glanced into the mug like someone gazing down the shaft of a well. "Did you spike this?" Laughing, she glanced up and managed a wink. When Nicolette tried to stand, she nearly tumbled off the stool. She laughed again.

Yikes. Too strong. *Note to self: too much chamomile* and *lemon balm.*

How had she become so bad at this? Had she been focusing so much of her attention on her animated toys that all her other witch-skills had withered on the vine?

Amber attempted to help Nicolette, but much like her daughter, once Nicolette felt a little more like her old self, she didn't want assistance.

"Oh, stop fussing," Nicolette said, waving her off.

Amber dropped her arms to her sides, reeling back. Her bottom lip wobbled slightly and she sunk her teeth into the soft flesh of her lip to keep it in place.

When Nicolette glanced at her, safely on her feet again, some of her manufactured good humor faded. "What's wrong, hon?" she said, brow creased.

"That … that was one of the last things Mel said to me the day … before she …"

Amber bit down harder on her lip, gaze focused on the ground. Then it was Nicolette's turn to comfort Amber, grabbing both her hands with her delicate, cold fingers.

"If I find out who did this to my baby, I'll wring their neck," Nicolette said softly but fiercely, giving Amber's hands a little squeeze. She sounded like Willow. "They'll have to answer to *me*," she said in a strong, even tone, revealing what was likely closer to the woman's usual personality when not weighed down by grief.

"Did she ever talk to you about anyone she had problems with?" Amber asked. "A coworker or a boyfriend?"

Nicolette scoffed, letting Amber go. The woman rested her hip against the counter and crossed her arms, facing Amber. "You knew Mel. I know I might be biased, but it was hard not to like her. She was just one of those people." She shrugged. "She left behind a string of heartbroken men, sure, but nothing that would result in anyone trying to hurt her."

"Not even Derrick Sadler?" Amber blurted. Her face immediately heated, not realizing until it was too late that Nicolette might not know about Derrick.

But Nicolette only laughed. "That sorry fool? No way. Melanie broke things off with him years ago. He wanted more than she could give him. I poo-pooed the relationship at first—I mean ... a married man? With my history?

"They met at one of those boring marketing conferences and were staying at the hotel where the conference was. One drink led to two, two led to five, and ... well," she said. "They saw each other on and off since then, but it was strictly a fling. Didn't mean anything. When he said he wanted to leave his wife for her, she said no. He got a bit stalkery and she got uncomfortable. He wouldn't leave her alone, so she went to HR and eventually got a rather hefty severance package to keep quiet about the affair. Then she quit and moved to Edgehill."

Amber blinked, trying to process all this. "Wait, so Derrick Sadler worked at Northwind Consultants too?"

"Mmhmm," Nicolette said. "He got a job there shortly after their initial hookup. It was one of those positions where he worked half the time in California and half here in Oregon—at least that's what Mel told me. I was never very clear on the details."

"If he went through all that trouble to track her down, and she didn't want to be with him, why did she move to Edgehill of all places?" Amber asked.

Nicolette cocked her head. "Why wouldn't she? She said she loved the quirky cat theme of the town. Liked the slower pace. It's far enough from California, and such a tiny place on the map that silly Derrick Sadler would *really* need to put in the work to find her. She moved here to start over."

Oh, Nicolette ...

"What?" Nicolette asked. "Why are you looking at me like that?"

"Because Derrick Sadler lives *here*," Amber said. "He and his wife have lived here for years."

Nicolette blinked once. Twice. Several times. "What?"

"I … I think *she* may have followed *him* here," Amber said.

Amber was starting to suspect that Melanie was more serious about Derrick than even Melanie was willing to admit.

"No, there's no way," Nicolette said, shaking her head. "Why would she lie to me about that? It doesn't … no."

Amber bit her bottom lip, unsure of what to say.

"There has to be something else going on here." The woman's expression hardened. "Do you think he's responsible for this?"

Amber held up her hands to show her innocence. "I don't know. I'm trying to figure it out. I want to know what happened to her as much as you do."

After a few moments of silence, Nicolette rubbed the spot between her eyebrows. Swayed a little. "I think I need to lie down. I've been … I haven't been able to sleep much since I got the news. I fall asleep for about an hour and then wake up screaming or crying. I just feel … tired now. So tired."

The hint of valerian root seemed to be doing *too* good of a job. Amber wondered if she should just throw her entire tincture collection out and start again from scratch.

"Do you want to lie down upstairs?" Amber asked. "It's quiet up there—as long as you don't mind cats."

The woman's smile was brief. "I told Chief Brown I would meet with him today. He said he could personally take me over to the morgue." She blew out a long breath. "My baby's been lying in a cold box for four days all by herself. I told them not to touch her, not to examine her, until I could get here. And yet, now that I'm actually *in* Edgehill …"

"What if you just take a short nap?" Amber said. "Chief Brown will understand if you need more time."

Nicolette nodded slowly. "Yes, maybe just a little bit of rest." Suddenly she looked as if she could topple over at any moment.

Amber helped her to the door that would lead her upstairs. Walking behind her, keeping a hand out just in case the valerian root fully kicked in and the woman fell asleep on her feet and tumbled into Amber, she inched after Nicolette. Thankfully, Alley and Tom decided today was the day to be perfect angels; they hopped off the bed and onto the window bench seat. Nicolette pitched forward onto the bed almost immediately, her rhythmic, slow breaths following soon after.

Amber sighed in relief.

When she was sure Nicolette was well and truly asleep, Amber scribbled a note and left it on the kitchen table, along with her cell phone number in case she needed to step out while Nicolette slept.

Amber told the cats to behave, and then she tiptoed back downstairs and into the shop. She'd forgotten to leave a message on her magicked blackboard that she would be unavailable for a few minutes, but she didn't find anyone wandering her store.

Nicolette's resemblance to Melanie was uncanny. It was like Melanie's ghost had walked into the Quirky Whisker. And now that ghost was sleeping on her bed.

Amber thought about how hard it must have been for

Nicolette to travel here alone for the sole purpose of identifying the body of her only daughter. Though Melanie had clearly lied to her mother about her relationship with Derrick, when Melanie had talked about her mother, she'd done so with such adoration. Nicolette had been a single mother for most of Melanie's life; Melanie's father had run off with the babysitter. Amber supposed that was why Melanie had lied about Derrick. By her own admission, Nicolette wasn't terribly sympathetic to infidelity, since infidelity had upended her own life.

Amber's thoughts drifted to Melanie—of her alone in the morgue, unclaimed and cold, in a metal box for days now.

Days without being examined *or* touched.

Her body still held clues to her death.

Could Amber find out the true cause of Melanie's death from Melanie herself? Amber's magic worked best with physical contact. She had never performed a spell on a corpse before, but she knew spirits, energies, and memories lingered in bodies for days after death. And said spirits, energies, and memories lingered in objects even longer. They often were fused into objects that were present at the height of emotion—or trauma.

As soon as Nicolette gave the okay, Melanie's body would be poked and prodded and cut open.

Amber shot a glance toward the door that led to her studio apartment, as if she expected Nicolette to come down the stairs and scold her for what she was thinking. Any good mother would tell her not to do this.

But Amber no longer had a mother and hadn't for a long time.

So Amber did a quick locator spell to find her cell phone—it was in a box of potpourri in the corner of the room; Amber was starting to wonder if pixies hid the device when she wasn't looking—added a "Be back in an hour!" to her magicked chalkboard, and quietly let herself out of her shop. She pulled on her coat as she walked, her flat boots quiet on the asphalt as she walked quickly to her car.

There was no time to waste. She had a morgue to sneak into.

CHAPTER 7

The Edgehill Coroner sat at the end of a quiet street about twenty-five minutes from the Quirky Whisker, on the border between Edgehill and Marbleglen. Next door to the coroner was a pizza place, and a gas station took up half the short block across the street. A wide green lawn stretched out in front of the coroner's office, dotted with a couple of tall, leafy trees that surely provided ample shade in the summer. The branches were mostly bare now.

It wasn't depressing, per se, but cheery didn't come to mind either.

The short, squat building was made of a tan-colored stone. Neutral. Nothing too flashy. The sign out front on the lawn was as short and squat as the building it sat in front of and made of the same neutral-colored stone, the words printed in golden brown. Amber had never paid much attention to the building before this.

When her parents died, there had been so little left of their bodies, an extensive analysis from a coroner had proved to not only be unnecessary, but close to impossible.

She turned onto Devon Rex Drive, passed the small driveway leading into the coroner's parking lot, and pulled to a stop several houses down. The office was at the edge of a sleepy residential neighborhood.

From her quick glance into the parking lot, she saw only two cars were there. Though death didn't have a schedule, Amber wondered if it was normally this quiet on a Saturday afternoon. One large, nondescript white van, and an older model, dark four-door car sat in the lot. Since Nicolette was due to come here sometime this afternoon, Amber had to assume at least one of those cars belonged to the coroner. She had to hope that the second one didn't belong to Chief Owen Brown.

Pulling up a search engine on her phone, she typed in "Edgehill Coroner." The man in charge was Dr. Fredrick Bunson and, from his picture, he looked like he was pushing sixty. A younger female coroner was listed along with two younger techs who were both female. Hours of operation were set as twenty-four hours, but reports could only be requested during typical work hours, Monday through Friday.

Amber craned her neck to catch what sight she could of the building and its parking lot from her vantage point down the street. Much of her view was blocked by the foliage and wooden fence circling the house, flush with the coroner's parking lot.

She needed to figure out who was in the building. They wouldn't let her see the body before Melanie's next of kin, especially since they were already expecting Nicolette. But if Melanie's body truly hadn't been handled much since she was brought here, Amber needed to get what clues she could from it. If only so the Susie Paulsons of the world would stop falsely accusing her.

Reaching into her bag, Amber pulled out her personal grimoire. She'd started it after her parents died, as every spellbook to the Blackwoods' name had been destroyed in the fire. Tinctures and tonics made up a large portion of the spellbook's beginning. Tonics were just as much about natural ingredients—making her a bit of a kitchen witch, like her aunt Gretchen—as they were about magic. Amber's tinctures got a boost in effectiveness when paired with an activation spell. In theory.

For most witches like Amber, learning a spell took practice with stating incantations. But the trick to mastering a spell didn't only lie in the words spoken; the intent of the spellcaster was just as important. When Amber tested out spells—mostly on her unsuspecting plastic creations—her intention might not be as clear as her words, causing the spell to fail. When a spell was conducted correctly on all levels, her magic—which she thought of as a physical thing that flowed through her—reacted. A properly uttered spell caused her magic to pour out of her like a wave. A botched spell made it knock around uncomfortably inside her like a trapped insect. Some spells she wrote never worked, no matter how hard she tried. Others worked immediately.

The section of her personal grimoire that was the most populated with spells—often ones she crafted on her own—were ones that required physical touch to spark a reaction in another person. There were contact spells for confusion; temporary blindness—either to a specific object or person, or total blindness; forgetfulness; mindless cooperation; a sudden desire to leave a room; sleep; and many others. Beyond needing to know who was inside the building—the more people she had active spells on at once usually affected how strong each subsequent spell would be—she needed to know what kind of security the place had. Were cameras pointing at all the doors?

What she needed was to reduce the population in the office down to one. She could spell old Dr. Bunson into sleep for an hour with little problem. Assuming she could get him alone.

Amber flipped a few more pages until she came to the handful of spells she could conduct with the aid only of a subject's voice and/or a personal item. Sometimes looking at a picture of the individual worked in a pinch. With spells conducted over distance, intent became even more important. If Amber was going to lace magic into her voice, rather than her touch, the person on the other end of the line had to believe her words. They had to let their guard down long enough for Amber's magic to sneak in and take hold.

Grabbing her phone again, Amber pulled up the website for the coroner's office and clicked on the staff page. Both of the younger women were assistants to the doctors. If the office had a secretary on staff who wasn't listed, Amber was screwed and would need to implement plan B.

Which currently didn't exist.

Taking a deep breath, Amber hit the "call now" button, then put the phone on speaker. She bit her lip and anxiously tapped her foot.

Please only be Dr. Bunson, please only be Dr. Bunson—

"Good afternoon, Edgehill Coroner's office. How may I help you?"

It was a young woman's voice. Dang it. Amber's gaze flicked down to the first of the two smiling young women on her phone.

"Yes, hello," Amber said, easing a slight Southern twang into her voice for reasons unknown even to herself. "Who do I have the pleasure of speaking with?"

"This is Ericka, ma'am. I'm the assistant to Dr. Bunson. He's getting ready to perform an autopsy and is unable to come to the phone at the moment. Can I help you?"

Amber swiped down a couple of times until the smiling face of Ericka appeared on her screen. The young woman was brunette, a straight-line fringe resting against the smooth skin of her forehead. Amber guessed she was in her mid-twenties, if not younger.

Staring at the photograph, Amber called her magic to attention, hoping it would help her even though she didn't have all the elements needed to perform such a spell. She sent her magic out; sent it twisting away from her and toward Ericka's voice. Though her magic was invisible to even Amber, she liked to picture it like a smoky tendril of blue. A tether between herself and her subject.

She pictured it sliding under the door of the office and into the lobby. Around a desk, up the back of a chair, over a shoulder, and into Ericka's mind, seeking the specific thing Amber asked of it.

Amber told her magic to locate Ericka's guilty pleasure. Her magic would help guide Amber's next words and would push her into asking what would get her closest to the answers she wanted. Sometimes Amber was at the mercy of her magic, too. Merely a puppet doing what was instructed of her.

"Well, I'm from the *Belhaven Tribune*," Amber said, suddenly losing control of her mouth, "and I wanted to find out what you'd recommend if I was sightseeing in your area." That odd Southern accent hung on for dear life.

Ericka remained silent. Amber held her breath, imagining the tendril of blue magic rummaging around in the young girl's head like a burglar riffling through drawers. Had Ericka thought the question so strange, she wouldn't reply? After all, who in her right mind called a coroner's office to ask for sightseeing tips?

A giggle bubbled out of Ericka, the sound shooting out of the phone's tiny speaker and echoing through Amber's car. "I have this really great place to recommend but ..." Her voice lowered and Amber instinctively huddled closer to her phone. "Can I confess something to you?"

"Of course," Amber said, the inexplicable Southern accent getting even twangier. "Locals always have the best information."

"Okay, so there's a place called Once and Floral that has ice cream to die for," Ericka said, then laughed. "Sorry, coroner humor."

Amber supplied a polite chuckle.

"Their lavender blackberry ice cream is absolutely sinful. But ... it's in Marbleglen."

Amber wanted to gasp at the traitor. The ice cream at Cat's Creamery was the best ice cream for thirty miles, but Amber's southern persona wouldn't know that. Amber opened another browser to look up Once and Floral and scrolled through to their menu. The lavender blackberry ice cream did look pretty good. The lavender and honey ice cream with raspberry swirls looked even better. It was paired with a platter of fresh-baked sugar cookies. Amber's mouth watered. "What's wrong with Marbleglen?"

"Oh, the people here are weird about the town because of our competing festivals," Ericka said. "So I try not to let anyone know how often I go over there. I mean, once a week is already bad enough."

Amber had one more trick up her sleeve and hoped her magic would still obey. While staring at Ericka's picture, Amber added another layer to the guilty pleasure spell. Her remaining magic pulsed under her skin, ready to be of use. "It sounds like you might want to get yourself some of that ice cream right now."

"Now?" Ericka laughed. "I have to be here to assist Dr. Bunson."

Pouring more of her magic into the spell, into convincing Ericka that she really needed to leave the office right now and head into Marbleglen, her voice suddenly took on a flat, almost robotic affectation. Something Amber had zero control over. "It's Saturday. You want a treat. I'm sure Dr. Bunson will forgive you for leaving if you bring some back for him. This will keep you from returning to Marbleglen this evening. You know you were going to go after work. You think about it all the time." Amber stared at the pictures of treats, imagining the cool ice cream on her tongue before sliding down her throat.

Ericka let out a sound that was somewhere between a purr and a whimper. "I'm sorry, but I have to go."

The call abruptly ended.

Amber turned in her seat and peered over the fence. She could only see part of the white van, but, within seconds, the dark-colored second car zoomed through the lot, made a left, and then a quick right, presumably now well on its way to cross the border into Marbleglen.

Which left Dr. Bunson alone in the office. Amber called on her magic, feeling it settle back into her. The slight thrum was still there, as her magic loved to be used, but it was more a steady heartbeat than an alien force. Amber was in control again.

Confident that she could get in to see Melanie now, Amber took a folded piece of paper out of her grimoire and stuffed it into her pocket. She threw the book into her glove box, tossed her phone into her purse, slung it over her shoulder, and did her best to look casual as she strode toward the coroner's office.

There were no glass eyes of cameras watching her from the eaves around the building's entrance, so she wouldn't have to worry about that, at least. But that didn't mean there wasn't at least one camera inside. She had to be alert.

The windows on the front of the building had drawn-closed blinds, and the glass of the front door was so dark, Amber could hardly make out anything beyond it. Letting herself in, she cautiously peeked her head inside the small lobby. She was relieved to find it empty. The inside reminded her a lot of a veterinarian's office. A large round reception desk took up most of the room, with small offices and two hallways snaking off behind it. She did a quick scan of the corners, trying not to make it obvious that she was searching for cameras.

Then she spotted a black dome housing a camera in the middle of the ceiling, directly above the circular reception desk. When she used her spell on Dr. Bunson, it couldn't be in this room.

"Hello?" she called out. "Hello ..."

No answer.

Taking a deep breath, she walked around the left side of the desk and down the first hallway. There were offices on both sides of the short, dead-end corridor—both doors were closed. Amber backtracked and went around the right side of the desk. The hallway here was almost identical to the first, but this one had an extra door at the end. As Amber moved toward it, her heart thundered in her chest. She wasn't sure if she was more nervous about being caught creeping around, or about seeing Melanie's lifeless body. Now that the reality of the situation started to sink in, Amber felt a little sick to her stomach.

Was she mentally prepared to see Melanie like this?

Amber reached the end of the hallway and stood before an unremarkable gray door with a single silver-colored doorknob. She hoped Dr. Bunson wasn't waiting on the other side.

After wiping her sweaty palms on her pants, Amber reached out and took the cool metal in her hand. She turned it. Unlocked. Mild disappointment rounded her shoulders. If it had been locked, she could just have gone home. Could have said she tried but there was nothing else for her to do.

She pulled the door open and cautiously poked her head inside. The hallway before her was stark white. And empty.

Amber crept in, flinching when, halfway down the little corridor, the door snicked shut. She held her breath, but no one came out to investigate the noise. There was only one door here, in the middle of the wall to her left. A small window rested at eye level and Amber peered through the reinforced glass, crisscrossed with small diamond shapes.

Inside was a white, sterile-looking room. Across from her, gray boxes were built into the wall in neat rows. Amber blew out a slow breath.

In the middle of the room stood a metal table on wheels. And, on top of that, was a form covered in a thick plastic sheet. Melanie. Amber was sure of it. Tears threatened to well in Amber's eyes, but she willed them back. This wasn't the time to cry.

Amber craned her neck to try and spot Dr. Bunson. Nothing to the right. And to the left—Amber jumped. Dr. Bunson, in what looked like a plastic parka, stood before a table, head down as he worked. Likely he was prepping something for Melanie's viewing, as well as the autopsy to follow immediately afterwards. The best results came from inspecting a body as close to death as possible, and Melanie had already been kept frozen for four days.

Without allowing herself to overthink it, Amber pushed open the door to the morgue.

Dr. Bunson turned at the sound, a question already leaving his mouth. "Any word from the chief or Mrs. Cole yet, Ericka? It's odd I haven't—" The rest of what he was going to say died on his lips when he realized it wasn't his assistant who'd just joined him.

"Amber Blackwood?" he asked. "What are you doing here?"

The lie came easy. "I was supposed to meet Nicolette Cole here. She said she wanted the extra moral support. There was no one manning the front, so I just came back here, thinking the viewing had already started."

Dr. Bunson pursed his lips. "No one is here yet, Miss Blackwood. It would be best if you wait out front. I'm sure Ericka just ran out to her car to fetch something."

"Does she drive a black car?" she asked. "I saw it leave as I pulled up."

His bushy gray eyebrows bunched together. "Are you sure? My, this is all very irregular."

Amber's gaze shifted of its own accord to the lump under the sheet on the rolling metal table.

"Why don't we head out into the lobby and make a few phone calls, hmm? It would be best to have everyone here before we get started," Dr. Bunson said, pulling off his gloves. He tossed them into a nearby trashcan and headed for her.

Amber quickly moved past him, to where he'd been standing before a table with a small desk chair in front of it. A quick scan of the work surface told her he'd been looking through Melanie's file.

"Miss Blackwood," he said, his tone chastising, as if Amber were a misbehaving child. Amber supposed she was, in a way. "Please follow me to the lobby."

She turned to him. His brows were pulled so tightly

together, they looked like one angry caterpillar crawling across his forehead. "Do you know what happened to her?" she asked.

The slight tremble to her voice softened his features. The angry caterpillar became two again. He sighed, as if he'd just remembered that sometimes he had to play therapist to grieving family and friends—even ones who burst into his workspace uninvited.

He closed the distance between them and grabbed her hand, patting the back of it with his free one. His grip was firm. Age spots dotted his skin. "I don't know what happened to her, but once her mother approves the autopsy, we can get started right away to figure it out."

The feel of his skin on hers woke up her magic. Contact was what she needed. And being here in this room with Melanie, with the grief and the anger bubbling under the surface once more, her magic was eager to be poured into another spell. Luckily for Amber—and quite unluckily for poor Dr. Bunson—she had perfected her sleep spell at a young age. As a teenage witch with an oftentimes annoying younger sister, putting each other to sleep had become a favorite pastime in the Blackwood household.

Only a single word and eye contact was needed for the spell now.

Gaze focused squarely on the blue eyes of Dr. Bunson, Amber said, "Sleep."

Almost immediately, the man's eyes rolled back in his head. She caught him before he hit the ground. He was heavier than he looked, and she struggled to get him into his waiting chair.

When she finally got him into it, his limbs splayed out, and head lolling back, she felt guilty.

But only a little.

Snapping her fingers by his ears several times, she waited for him to react. He let loose a snorting snore instead. Out cold. Amber tossed her purse onto the table with Melanie's records—she'd check those out afterward, if she still had time—and then slowly made her way to the slab where her friend's body waited.

Steeling herself, Amber grabbed a corner of the sheet by the head of the table, counted to three, and flipped the plastic back. A choked sound tore from Amber's throat, a sound she silenced with a hand over her mouth as she laid eyes on Melanie's pale face. Her lips were tinged the same sickly blue Amber had seen in the snapshot of memory she'd pulled from Chief Brown.

Oh Melanie, who did this to you?

Amber didn't have time to waste. She had to get this over with before someone else showed up to the office.

Knowing the sensation would haunt her for a while—if not forever—Amber lifted the plastic further until she found Melanie's hand. She took the cold, hard flesh in her own, ignoring her urge to recoil. Her toes curled in her boots. All she could think of were movies about reanimated corpses. If Melanie came back to life suddenly and sat up, Amber would surely pass out.

Using her free hand, she pulled the folded piece of paper out of her pocket. It was a spell for recalling memories, the same one she'd used on Connor and Chief Brown, but since the life force had left Melanie's body, she'd need to modify it on the fly. Amber had never used a spell on a dead body before, so she had no way of knowing if it would work. It wasn't like she had an endless supply of corpses to practice on.

Reading the spell over several times, tweaking where necessary, she closed her eyes, then recited the spell from memory, still holding onto Melanie's cold, lifeless hand. She waited. Nothing happened. Amber cracked open an eye. Neither Melanie nor Dr. Bunson stirred.

When a spell was fussy, it was often due to intention error more than spell-craft error.

Letting a slow breath out of her nose, Amber reevaluated her motivation for being here. She wanted to know the truth. That was it. Pure and simple.

Her magic felt sluggish. Reluctant.

Truth *wasn't* the only thing she wanted to gain from this spell?

Amber thought about the way the chief had looked at her with disdain the day Melanie had died. The way Susie Paulson had accused Amber of drugging her customers to keep them loyal. How Amber had offered Connor a cup of tea and he'd declined after scanning her shelves of tinctures.

Amber wanted to do this spell to clear herself of suspicion. She wanted to prove to everyone—and herself—that she had nothing to do with this. Because some little, faraway part of her wondered if Owen Brown was right to accuse her. What if some combination of ingredients, plus the activation spell, really *had* harmed Melanie? What if she'd truly been sick and Amber's tincture had made it worse?

The intention for this spell was as much about clearing Amber's name as it was about finding the truth.

Her magic practically sang beneath her skin.

Scanning the words of the spell one more time, Amber shut her eyes and said the words, her voice ringing out in the quiet room.

Almost immediately, jagged pieces of images filled Amber's head. But "images" wasn't quite right. These were feelings. Residual emotions trying to give themselves visual form. Trying to explain themselves to Amber. Sensations she felt and heard, followed by the associated emotion expressed in a burst of color behind her closed lids.

A knock on a door, followed by the bright burst of yellow relief.

The scratch of tissues on a raw nose, followed by the warm orange bloom of appreciation when someone wrapped a blanket around cold shoulders.

The tinkling bells of welcome, followed by the comforting blue of friendship.

The joy of being home, followed by the creeping, crawling black of an intruder.

The quick, sharp sting of a bug bite, followed by the seeping, invading red of muscles tensing, of a stomach heaving.

The cold, hard surface of tile and the rush of water.

A swipe of a towel across mouth and neck and hands.

The sensation of being dragged like a child's doll across a hard floor.

Something small and fragile being placed in a hand, fingers forced to wrap around the object.

The blinding, piercing white of betrayal.

Amber stumbled back, breath coming in deep, labored gasps, hands pressed to her chest. Melanie's lifeless hand flopped over the side of the table, curled fingers beckoning Amber to come back. To take her hand again.

No. No, Amber had to get out of here.

She shoved the mangled note with the spell on it, the ink smudged in places from Amber's sweaty palm, back into her pocket. She hurried past the still-sleeping form of Dr. Bunson and snatched up her purse, flinging it back over her shoulder. Amber couldn't have cared less about Melanie's records now. Amber had seen enough.

Glancing back at Melanie, she found her still partially uncovered. Letting out a whimper, Amber quickly walked back to fling the sheet back over her friend. Her stomach clenched.

Amber needed to get out.

She wrenched open the door of the morgue and speed walked down the blindingly white hallway. The flash of images and the bursts of color kept replaying in her head. The last one most of all. The word echoing in her head with every quick footfall. Betrayal, betrayal, betrayal.

Plus the realization that not only had Melanie been killed by someone she knew, but the person had *placed* her in the living room where she'd been found. It hadn't been an accidental killing. It hadn't been murder fueled by passion that flared up at the wrong moment, resulting in a horrible mistake.

This had been premeditated. And someone had tried to clean it up—and possibly deflect suspicion onto Amber. Just as Connor had speculated.

Ericka still hadn't returned from Marbleglen, so Amber was met with no opposition as she practically sprinted across the lobby to the exit. Amber was thankful: she wasn't sure she'd be able to answer even the simplest of questions in the state she was in now.

Which made it especially unfortunate that the moment she bolted out the dark-glassed front door of the coroner's office, she smacked right into Chief Owen Brown.

CHAPTER 8

Chief Brown's strong hands clamped down on Amber's arms, pinning them to her sides. She knew he'd done so on instinct—she'd just careened into him, after all—but a wave of panic washed over her nonetheless. What would he do now that he had her?

His blond hair was curly and unruly, just like little Sammy's, and his bright blue eyes scanned her face. A face that no doubt telegraphed guilt. Amber would make a terrible poker player; her tells were too obvious.

He unhanded her and took a step back, crossing his arms. He wore his uniform, the long-sleeved dark blue shirt bunching up a little at the elbows, the fabric strained. Was his body going soft now that he lived in Edgehill? Was his uniform ill-fitting in the wake of a quieter, slower life? Jutting a chin in her direction, he said, "And where are you off to in such a hurry?"

"Uhh … home?" Her voice cracked. Really, she should just wear a sign that said, "Hi! Ask me about my guilt!" She needed to get a grip. Clearing her throat, she said, "I heard Nicolette Cole was coming here to view the body today and I wanted to be here."

"Bit presumptuous to show up unannounced." One of

Owen's dirty blond brows arched. "How did you hear about the viewing?"

Amber wasn't sure how to answer that. "People gossip."

He narrowed his eyes at her. "You have an uncanny knack of knowing things before anyone else does, Miss Blackwood. Why is that?"

Amber could only assume he meant Melanie's death and the fact she'd known about it before the chief showed up to crassly break the news. "I told you. Kimberly Jones called me after she—"

"That was one example of many."

Amber's brows furrowed.

Chief Brown checked his watch. "Why don't we take a little trip down to the station?"

Her heart thudded. "Am I in trouble for something?"

In trouble. As if she were a little kid again. Witch or not, Amber had always felt uneasy around authority figures.

"I'd like to have you in for questioning. We're overdue. Standard procedure and all that," he said. "Take a ride with me down there, we'll have a chat, and I'll bring you back in an hour. Perhaps I'll have heard from Nicolette Cole by then."

Declining his "offer" would do her no favors. She nodded.

He walked her to his squad car and opened the back door for her, keeping his gaze focused on something over her shoulder, like he couldn't bear to look at her. Really? He was going to make her ride in the back like a common criminal? Sighing to herself, she ducked inside.

After closing the door, instead of climbing into the driver's seat, the chief headed into the coroner's office. He likely wanted to let Dr. Bunson know that he still hadn't heard from Melanie's mother and that he'd be tied up for at least an hour while he talked to Amber. How long would it take the chief to find the doctor passed out in his chair? The spell wasn't due to wear off for at least another half hour, and Amber couldn't use her magic to wake him up before then without direct contact. Nothing would be able to wake the doctor early save for another spell.

Ten minutes later, the chief strode back out. Amber couldn't read his expression. Then again, the partition separating her from the front seat, as well as the tinted glass of the windows, wasn't conducive to seeing—well, much of anything.

Sitting with her knees together and her hands folded neatly in her lap, Amber put on her most innocent expression. The chief got into the driver's seat and slammed the door so hard, the car rocked gently. He turned abruptly in his seat to peer at her through the mesh partition. Lip curling slightly, he said, "What's wrong with Dr. Bunson?"

"What do you mean?"

A red tint inched up his throat and into his cheeks. Perhaps it wasn't best to tick off the armed officer.

"I mean," she said quickly, "I don't know that anything is *wrong* with him. He's an older guy; he probably gets sleepy often."

The red hue colored his entire face now. If he were a cartoon character, steam would be billowing from his ears.

"I found the place empty when I went in," she added. "I went looking for the doctor, since I assumed he had to be in the building somewhere, and I found him in the morgue, asleep in his chair. I … I know I shouldn't have, but I looked under the sheet. Curiosity got to me. I ran out of there so fast because I wasn't mentally prepared to see my friend like that. I've never seen a dead body before." Tears welled in her eyes. True, genuine tears. She dropped her gaze to her lap. "I took off without even trying to wake the doctor again."

When several more seconds ticked by without the chief uttering a word, she hazarded a glance up. He stared at her, mouth pursed. He was a little less red in the face now, at least. Abruptly, he turned back around and started up the car.

The ride to the police station was silent and charged. There had always been tension between her and the chief, but aside from his trips to the Quirky Whisker on toy-demonstration days, the random sighting in town, and him stopping by her booth with his family during the Here and Meow, she didn't interact with the man that often. It had mostly been hateful glares from afar. The occasional snippy comment.

But since Melanie's death, he'd become outright menacing.

"Did I do something to make you hate me, chief?" she asked, before she realized she was going to say it out loud.

All she got for an answer was his knuckles turning white as he gripped the steering wheel more tightly.

A row of diagonally parked police cars were lined in front of the station. The chief wordlessly parked, then escorted her up the short flight of stairs and into the front of the tan-brick building. The offices for the *Edgehill Gazette* were only a few doors down. Amber hoped Connor Declan wasn't watching. What would he think of her now?

She wasn't sure why she cared what he thought.

The inside of the station smelled like old rubber and even older coffee. The flecked tile under her feet was cracked in places, the grout a dark brown. To the left, a tired-looking receptionist with a head full of frizzy, overly teased blonde hair sat behind a worn-wood wall, a large rectangle cut out of the middle. No glass separated her from anyone who might stroll through the door, but given the no-nonsense look she angled Amber's way, Amber figured anyone who walked in and gave her hell would likely regret it.

Chief Brown acknowledged the receptionist with a wave of his hand, then he guided Amber to the right. They passed a small seating area furnished with an old brown couch, a pair of mismatched plastic chairs, and a low table stacked with magazines sure to be at least a decade old. A water cooler hummed softly in a corner.

The station was quiet save for the chatter of voices behind the closed doors they passed, and the ringing of a phone in the distance. Owen stopped at the third door to the right and opened it, gesturing for her to enter. She cautiously stepped inside.

The room was small, with only space for a small table wedged into a corner and two chairs. Amber wondered if it had originally been a broom closet that had gotten repurposed as an interrogation room. Perhaps the small quarters were meant to drive criminals mad.

Amber took a seat, clutching her purse to her chest as if it were a life raft.

The chief had yet to sit. "Would you like water or coffee?"

Amber startled. It was the first thing he'd said to her since they left the parking lot of the coroner's office. "Water, please."

He nodded once and left the room, closing the door behind him. Giving the room a quick once-over, she located a mounted camera in the corner behind her head, as well as one above the door. She wondered how long he'd keep her in here by herself. Would he be in a room somewhere, watching her squirm? Waiting for her to crack?

It wasn't long before her leg started to bounce.

By the time Chief Brown returned, Amber had gone from scared to bored to borderline angry. What was it about her that made him treat her like this? Did he truly believe she was a suspect?

According to her cell phone, it had taken a full half hour before he returned with a cup of water. She knew in the back of her mind that she could have walked out whenever she wanted. She wasn't under arrest.

"Sorry about that," he said, placing the cup of likely room-temperature water in front of her. The slap of a legal pad onto the table's surface in front of him made her flinch. He sat in the only other chair and leaned back, one leg kicked out. He folded his hands on his stomach. "A rather interesting phone call came in while I was getting your water. I had to take it."

Whatever. She'd seen enough cop shows to know not to take the bait. "So why am I here?"

The corner of his mouth ticked up in the ghost of a smile. "Just wanted to get an official statement about what happened the day of Melanie Cole's death."

Suppressing a sigh, Amber went through everything she'd

told him four days ago. He took notes this time. He asked her the same questions and she gave him the same answers. He asked again what was in the vial she'd given Melanie, and she explained—again—what passionflower and valerian root were used for.

Dropping his pen onto his scribbled-on pad, he scooted a little closer and rested his arms on the edge of the table, leveling his steady gaze at her. "Now, Miss Blackwood, you say you didn't give Melanie Cole anything other than natural ingredients, correct? Just a little something to help her sleep?" Amber nodded. "I find it very curious that Nicolette Cole called here about twenty minutes ago saying she was running late because she'd fallen asleep unexpectedly at your apartment. Care to explain why people always seem to be strangely incapacitated around you? Dr. Bunson. Nicolette. Her daughter …"

Amber's cheeks heated. She realized how bad this looked. "Nicolette came to see me and she was in such a state, I wanted to give her something to calm her down. It … relaxed her so much that it made her drowsy. I said she could sleep it off at my place. That's it."

"And while Mrs. Cole was sleeping, you decided to swing by the morgue without her because …"

Amber didn't have an answer.

"Because, to me, it sounds like you realized Mrs. Cole was going to authorize an autopsy, which meant the evidence of Melanie's cause of death could be discovered. You drugged her mother, placed a bogus call to Dr. Bunson's assistant to get her out of the office, drugged the doctor, and then what was the plan? Remove evidence from the body? We still haven't located Melanie's cell phone. Do you happen to know where it is?" He paused for a moment, arching a brow at her. "Evidence tampering is a felony, Miss Blackwood."

Chief Brown said all this with such calm, with such an even tone, that some part of Amber wondered if it all made sense. Was *he* a witch? Was he lacing magic into his words to convince her of a lie because it suited his purposes?

"I know you and I have butted heads a bit," he said, "but I'm here to help you. You tell me what really happened, and I'll make sure you're taken care of, okay?"

Taken care of. Ha.

No, he wasn't a witch. He just wanted to believe she was guilty.

Amber clutched her purse to her chest. "It wasn't me. I swear it."

He shook his head, keeping only one arm resting on the table while the other hand ran through his hair. "I'm trying to help you, Miss Blackwood, but I can't do that if you don't talk to me."

What was she supposed to tell this man? That she went to the morgue to use a thought-reveal spell on her friend's corpse?

Amber thought back to the string of sensations and colors she'd pulled from Melanie's body. A hiding assailant. An attack in the dark.

"I didn't do anything to her," Amber said. "Plus, breaking and entering really isn't my style. I wouldn't be cowardly enough to sneak up on someone, especially not a friend."

The sharp sting of a bug bite.

114

What if that sensation hadn't actually been a bug bite, but something else? A syringe? A needle full of poison that had been injected into Melanie? Amber absently touched her own neck, trying to rub away the phantom ache.

It was someone Melanie had known. Someone who either had already had access to her house, or someone who had known how to get in. Someone who—

A warm hand landed on her forearm. Her gaze snapped to the chief's face, to his searching blue eyes. He said something to her, likely another plea for her to confide in him.

But she couldn't hear him. Because his skin on hers woke up her magic, making it trill and thrum. Thought-reveal? No, he was too calm now, too in control of his emotions. She needed the truth from him. There was no time to craft a spell specific to her needs. No time to consult her grimoire. Truth spells were tricky. But she could do one for a simple truth. One that would only yield a yes or a no in response.

Gathering her magic, she instructed it to hurtle toward Chief Brown when she commanded it. And then she asked her question, her forearm warm where his hand met skin. "Do you truly believe I'm guilty of killing Melanie?"

"No," he said without hesitation. It was the total conviction with which he said it that startled him the most, she thought.

He yanked his hand back.

"If you don't think I'm responsible, then why are you trying to convince me to confess?"

The red tint was starting to creep into his face again. His mouth bunched into a pucker. Leaning toward her, one elbow on his knee, he squinted slightly. Voice low, he said, "How did you do that?"

"Do what?"

He blew out a breath but didn't change his posture other than to drop his gaze to the old freckled tile beneath their feet. Finally, he tipped his head back up to look at her. "You asked me earlier if you'd done something to make me … dislike you."

Amber swallowed but kept quiet.

"Like and dislike are irrelevant," he said, his voice still low. Almost too low; she had to inch forward to hear him. "But trust? That's more important. And I don't trust you, Miss Blackwood. Strange, unexplained things happen around you too often. You might think no one sees, but I do. I watch. I pay attention. Something here isn't right."

Swallowing again, she said, "Which means you don't actually have evidence of anything. Am I free to go?"

He finally sat up, back against the chair. He crossed his arms, working his jaw as he stared at her. "You're free to go."

Amber jumped to her feet. "I can find my own way back to my car, thank you."

She crossed the short distance to the door; the chief didn't move. Even after she'd pulled the door open and let out some of the stifling air trapped in that tiny room, he didn't budge.

Yet, mere moments from her escape, Chief Brown said, "Miss Blackwood?"

Glancing over her shoulder, she waited for him to speak.

He turned in his seat then, focusing that level gaze at her. "I'll be in touch. Don't leave town."

She nodded once, then scurried out the door.

CHAPTER 9

Amber hurried down the hall of the stale-smelling police station. The sour-faced receptionist sat at her wooden box of a desk, her flat eyes watching Amber as she bee-lined for the door. The woman sat stone-still save for the slow, methodical motion of her jaw as she chewed gum. Or tobacco. She looked like the type.

Amber had just passed the small waiting area to her left when a tall, gangly officer came barreling out of a room up ahead, a fistful of papers held over his head as he jogged down the hall. His expression implied he'd just found gold. Amber had to quickly sidestep the man who didn't even seem to see her, excited as he was about his discovery.

"Chief!" the gangly guy said, past Amber now. "We got the information off Cole's phone!"

Feeling as if someone had just glued her boots to the floor, Amber stopped dead in her tracks. She turned around, immediately making eye contact with Chief Brown.

Before she knew it, she was stomping back toward the chief. "You had her cell phone this whole time and yet questioned me as if I purloined it from her *dead body*?"

"There's no need for SAT words here, *Amber*," he snapped.

Then the chief pursed his lips and his gaze shot over her shoulder.

Amber glanced behind her to see a man and two young children standing wide-eyed in the lobby. "Oh, so now you're only concerned about false accusations when you have an audience?"

"Get back in here," the chief hissed, grabbing the gangly officer by the elbow and yanking him into the tiny, claustrophobic room Amber had just fled. She stayed rooted in the hallway. "Any day now, Miss Blackwood!" he called from inside.

Amber stomped into the room, closing the door behind her.

Chief Brown gestured to the chair she'd only just vacated and she plopped back into it, purse once again clutched to her chest. This time, the tight grip was due to annoyance rather than mild fear.

The gangly officer, who, on closer inspection, looked like he couldn't be more than twenty, danced a bit from foot to foot, sheets of paper still clutched in his fist. "I didn't mean … I was just …"

The chief sighed, then rubbed a forefinger up and down between his eyes. "Just sit down, Carl."

The young cop slunk into the only other available chair and placed the mangled stack of papers on the table, running his hands down the length of his pants.

"Carl here is new to the force," the chief supplied.

Carl leaned forward and offered a long-fingered hand to Amber to shake. When she did, he gave her hand a firm pump with his clammy one. "I started on Monday." He grinned, revealing honest-to-goodness braces.

Amber shot a dismayed look at the chief; Carl looked like he belonged in the locker-lined halls of Edgehill High, not the police station.

"His mother has been on the force for a decade," the chief said, as if that explained anything. He started to say something else, then thought better of it and snapped his mouth shut. Amber and Carl waited in awkward silence while Chief Brown paced the small room. After half a lifetime, he stopped and looked at Carl and Amber in turn. "I'm under intense pressure to solve this case. You cannot imagine the number of tips flooding our systems since the day Melanie was found. You wouldn't think Edgehill could rival some of the bigger cities I've worked in when it comes to the reaction to a homicide but, well …"

"People here like to talk," Amber said. "And they like to weasel into everyone's business. So when something like *this* happens—something that just doesn't happen here? People are going to be in a frenzy trying to solve the case. I'm sure every little thing anyone knows or *thinks* they know about Melanie has been called in."

The chief eyed her, rubbing his chin.

"That's right on the money," Carl said, nodding vigorously. "I'm not allowed out in the field or anything yet. I was super bummed about that, but my mom said it's good for me to learn how to do paperwork and stuff, you know? Half of an officer's job is deskwork. She said it would be pretty boring for a while, since not much happens here, and I should cherish this time while I can—to really soak it all in. But then that lady was poisoned and *hoo boy*! The phone won't stop ringing. I swear

I've talked to half the town in, like, three days. Everyone has a story and a theory."

"Do *you* have one?" Amber asked.

The chief groaned. "Please don't encourage him to speculate, Miss Blackwood. That's not good police—"

"I think it was that guy she was getting it on with," Carl said, either not hearing the chief or not caring. "That guy who's married to that hot lady ... Brittany? Nancy?"

"Whitney?" Amber said.

Carl snapped his long fingers and pointed at Amber. "Yep, her. Total babe. I think her husband killed Melanie to keep the affair a secret. But, I mean, everyone already knew about the affair, right? I mean everyone who calls is like, 'Well, you know she was having an affair with a married man, don't you?' The first time I got a call like that, I was like, 'No way!' but it's not shocking anymore. Everyone and their mom knows at this point. Poor Whitney, though. Maybe she'll let me pick up the pieces of her broken heart, you know what I mean?" He winked suggestively.

"All right, that's it, Chatty Cathy," the chief said. "Out you go. I need to talk to Miss Blackwood."

Carl's head swiveled toward Chief Brown as if he'd forgotten they had company. "Oh, okay. Yeah, boss. You got it. Sure thing." He got to his feet and reached for the mangled papers on the table.

"Uh uh! Leave those. I'll take care of that," the chief said. "Why don't you go man the phones?"

"Sure, sure!" Carl said, waving at Amber as he headed for the door. He pulled it open and was just about to leave when he looked back at her and offered a small smile. "I'm real sorry about your friend, Miss Blackwood."

Something twisted in Amber's chest. Then the boy was gone, the door shut behind him.

Chief Brown sat in Carl's vacated chair and heaved another sigh. "He's a good kid, but he's going to drive me to an early retirement."

Amber blinked. "He seems eager to help."

"Oh sure," he said. "But he's more like a puppy that's likely to pee on your shoes in excitement."

Amber wasn't sure what was happening here. Was the chief actually treating her like a fellow human? Was he confiding in her? She was suddenly too scared to say anything else and break the spell she hadn't cast.

He ran a hand through his hair, his gaze focused on the middle distance. It was then that Amber saw how dark the bags under his eyes were. Exhausted wasn't an adequate enough word.

He seemed to come back to himself suddenly, giving his head a shake. "I … apologize … for implying you had her cell phone when it had been in our possession."

Oh right. Now she remembered that this guy was a jerk who hated her. "Why *did* you imply it, especially when you admitted yourself that you don't think I'm guilty?"

He sat forward, elbows on his knees, hands clasped in front of him. His gaze was focused on the ground. Without looking at her, he said, "Do you remember that potluck lunch a few days after I started as the chief here?"

Amber hadn't expected that and felt her head cock to the

side like a curious cat. She thought about that for a moment. "Yeah. It was at Balinese Park, wasn't it?"

"Right," he said, eyes still downcast. "We were all set up near the pond. It was a nice time. A really warm welcome for a guy new to town. It was near the end of the festivities and everyone was a little sun-drunk and in food comas, so no one saw the little girl run away from her parents, chasing a duck."

It was coming back to her now and heat flooded Amber's cheeks.

"The duck was startled and started running, so the girl started running too. Full tilt on tiny legs. She tumbled down the side of that little hill and started sliding toward the pond. I was on my feet almost immediately and running for her, trying to catch her before she went into the water. Just seconds before she slid in headfirst, she was yanked back like someone grabbed her shirt and pulled her away. But I was the only one anywhere near her. I didn't touch her."

Amber remembered the yelps of concern from everyone who'd realized, too late, that not only was the two-year-old girl *not* with her play group, but moments from slipping under the murky green water of the pond. Amber recalled how people had leapt to their feet when they had seen Chief Brown sprinting after the girl.

Amber had known he wasn't going to make it to little Maddie. So, when everyone was preoccupied, she had uttered an incantation and yanked the girl to safety with the aid of her magic. Owen Brown had been met with a wild cheer when he'd walked up the slight incline with the little girl in his arms. Maddie had looked delighted at all the attention, no worse for wear save for the grass stains down the front of her frilly yellow dress. Her mother had rushed up to him and taken her daughter, using her free arm to hug the man. People had run over to pat him on the back and shake his hand and tell him how sure they were that he was *just* what Edgehill needed.

But for some reason, his gaze—brows pulled together—had kept finding Amber's. Had he seen something? Sometimes when she muttered spells, her lips moved, like she was silently singing along to a song on the radio. There was no way he could have known anything … magical … had happened. Still, his scrutiny from across the group of new fans and busybody townspeople had set her on edge. So, during a moment when he *wasn't* watching her, she'd slipped away.

She supposed fleeing had made her look even more suspicious.

His eyes, bright and blue, met hers now. "How do you explain that?"

"Maybe it just looked that way," she said. "Maybe her foot caught on something and slowed her down so she could stand on her own and—"

He proceeded to mention four other instances where something unexplained had happened in town, only for him to discover soon afterward that Amber had been there. "I don't know if you have a sixth sense that draws you to things. I don't know if you do some kind of … voodoo to make things happen …"

She laughed. Mostly because he clearly neither understood witchcraft nor voodoo. "Sorry … I'm … I'm not sure what you're trying to say right now."

He sat up straighter, gaze flicking to the stack of papers

Carl had left lying on the table. Melanie's cell-phone records. Amber wondered if the person who had been hiding in Melanie's house with a readied syringe had called Melanie that day. Were there incriminating text messages between her and Derrick Sadler?

"I'm saying you have an uncanny knack of ... knowing things," the chief said, pulling Amber back into the conversation. "Of having miraculous things happen around you. I don't trust it ... or you ... but ..." Sighing, he said, "I ... I can't believe I'm saying this, but I might need someone like you to help me with this case. I've never worked with a psychic before, and I'm not even sure that's the right label for you, but I need all the help I can get. I read that psychics can, I don't know, manipulate energy? So maybe that's how you saved Maddie from the pond by—"

But Amber had stopped listening. A psychic? He thought she was a *psychic*? Amber supposed it was as close as he was going to get without truly veering into the land of fantasy. Plus, psychics and police were known to work together. Perhaps this was the best explanation his mind could come up with. The most palatable possibility.

"How can I help?" she asked, cutting off his rambling.

He sputtered, clearly thrown off by the interruption. "Really? After ... all this?"

"If we're being honest, I don't care for you either," she said. "But I want to know what happened to Melanie just as much as you do. So if that means we need to form an alliance—you with your resources and me with my ... psychic abilities—then so be it." She held out a hand to him, elbow resting on her purse.

He eyed her hand warily, as if it were a live snake that might bite him. Then he reached out and shook it. "Okay. Some ground rules? I decide how much information you get. Sometimes there'll be things I can't share with you. I can't give you any records to take home or anything like that. And I don't want you snooping around, harassing potential witnesses, unless you and I discuss it first. Got all that?"

Amber chewed on her bottom lip, assessing him.

Leaning back a little in his chair, he jutted his chin at her. "What?"

"What changed?" she asked. "Ten minutes ago, you told me not to leave town, like I was some kind of flight risk. Why do you suddenly want to work with me?"

"When you left the room, something you said about the assailant occurred to me." His gaze momentarily shifted to the phone records. "The screen on the outside of Melanie's bedroom window—the one at the back of the house—had been pried off and discarded in the bushes. There were smudges in the dust on the windowsill that clearly indicate someone climbed in through that back window. We found a few dried leaf crumbs in odd places in her bedroom—leaves that are found on the tree behind her house, but not in front."

"So someone *did* break in!"

He nodded. "And we guess that someone broke in while she was visiting you at your shop. We think they hid in her house and waited for the right time to pounce." His brows pulled together, eyeing her like she was a bug under glass. Something to inspect. "Something else you just seemed to ... know."

Amber wasn't sure how to properly act like a psychic, so

she just shouldered right on past that. "It had to be someone who knew her house layout well enough to know where to hide and then ambush her."

"There are no defensive wounds on Melanie's body," he said. "Ambush is a strong word."

The phantom sting in her neck returned and she rubbed at the spot, the retrieved memory still strong even if Melanie had shared it after death.

"Are you …" His gaze shifted from her eyes to her neck and back again. "Are you getting one of your … senses?"

Amber did her best not to burst out laughing. The poor man really had no clue about any of this. Hoping she wasn't insulting psychics everywhere, she said, "Yes. I … I'm sensing neck pain of some kind. Maybe you can ask Dr. Bunson to check her neck for puncture wounds? Right side, about an inch from her earlobe."

The chief's familiar look of disdain returned, wrinkling his forehead. Had Amber taken things too far? Would details like that make her look like a legit psychic or a legit suspect?

"You're the real deal," he said, shaking his head in disbelief. "The crime scene photographer actually spotted the puncture wound the day Melanie's body was discovered, as the wound was … bleeding slightly."

Amber clenched her jaw.

"That detail hadn't been released to the public," he said. "If Betty Harris hadn't corroborated your story about when you were at your shop—because she was at hers, too—you'd be my top suspect."

So *that* was why he was begrudgingly confiding in her now. Amber would have to thank Betty later.

"Can you tell me what she was injected with?" he asked. "Any … sense … of whether or not the assailant was male or female?"

Amber shook her head. "I know that whatever she was injected with made her muscles tense and made her stomach sick. She was bathed after the fact, to clean up the mess, then placed in the living room. But I don't know what she was injected with or who did it."

The chief nodded as if none of this fazed him. Either his team had already figured this much out, or he was in cop mode, giving away nothing. Clearly, his poker face was far superior to hers.

Her attention shifted to the stack of papers on the table, left there by Carl. "What do you hope to find in those?"

The chief finally picked them up and folded the small stack in half, neither looking at them nor handing them over. "Don't know yet. If there's anything in the report I need clarification on—*after* I've had a chance to go over it—we can discuss it then."

Which, of course, made her desperate to see the report now.

"You asked Carl what his theory was," he said, shifting her attention back to him and away from the folded sheets of paper in his hands. "What's yours?"

"You also told me not to encourage speculation because it's not good police work," Amber countered.

The chief almost—*almost*—smiled. "Well, good thing for both of us, you're not a police officer."

Amber wasn't sure if she was supposed to be offended by that or not.

Thinking about the growing list of suspects, Amber had to admit that Carl's favorite was at the top of her list, too. "I think Derrick Sadler is a definite possibility."

"Oh?" he asked. "Poison is more of a woman's method, you know."

Amber nodded. "Maybe he chose poison to throw people off."

"Maybe," the chief conceded. "Why do you like him for it?"

Amber hesitated.

"Oh, don't clam up on me now, Miss Blackwood."

Sighing, she told him about the bogus email sent to Derrick about needing accounting advice, as well as Derrick's response. "It seems a little fishy that he claims he didn't even *know* Melanie, doesn't it?" she said.

"Not necessarily," the chief said. "Sure, his affair with Melanie might have been one of Edgehill's worst-kept secrets, but that doesn't mean Derrick knew the rest of the town knew. He could be trying to keep it from getting out. It's also possible Whitney wasn't aware the affair was happening."

Amber remembered the way Whitney's demeanor had changed when Amber had brought up the subject of Melanie's mystery man. Even if Whitney hadn't known about the affair, she'd known *something*. And it was a sore subject she had little to no desire to discuss.

"So you *don't* like Derrick for it?" she asked.

"Oh, I didn't say that," he said. "But I'm not one for speculation." The almost-smile almost appeared again.

"Do you think he's dangerous?" Amber asked. "Should I not meet with him?"

"You're meeting him at his office, aren't you?" When she nodded, he said, "No, I don't think he's dangerous. If anything, he's a calculated killer, not a reactive one."

Amber wasn't sure why the chief thought that would be comforting.

"I think you should keep the meeting as planned," he said. "How would you feel about having a set of questions to work into the conversation, to see how he reacts?"

"You want me to be an informant?" How had she gone from trading wary looks with this man to him asking her to help him with an investigation?

"Would that be a problem?"

"Well, no," she said, honestly feeling a little trill of excitement bubble in her core at the idea of working with police to not only solve a murder, but to solve one that had such a personal connection to her.

"Excellent," he said. "I'm currently chasing a few leads in regards to Mr. Sadler. If something comes up between now and Wednesday that tips my suspicions further into his corner, would you be up for wearing a wire during your chat with him?"

Amber blew out a long, slow breath. "Sure."

Good gravy, what had she gotten herself into?

CHAPTER 10

Amber was startled awake on Sunday morning by her land-line ringing. She stumbled out of bed, dislodging Tom—who yowled in protest—and plucked the phone out of its cradle after the third ring.

"Hello?" she said, her voice froggy even to her own ears.

"Oh gosh, did I wake you?"

It took Amber a second to recognize the voice. Nicolette Cole. Suddenly Amber felt more awake. "Yes, but it's okay. What's up, Nicolette?"

Amber peered at the wall clock. It was just after 7:00 a.m. Ugh. Why?

"I … gosh, I'm sorry," she said. "I tried to convince myself to go back to Melanie's house last night and I just … I couldn't. So I got a hotel room, but I haven't been able to sleep here either."

Amber frowned. "Is there anything I can do? You can always stay here. It's tiny, but I can sleep on the couch."

"Oh no, I don't want to put you out," she said. "I would … the police said it would be okay for me to go back and collect some of Melanie's things. I haven't decided what to do with the property itself yet, but I'd like to have some of her belongings to take back with me." She paused for so long,

Amber wondered if she'd hung up. "Would you go with me? I just don't think I can go there by myself."

Amber felt sick about going there, but the desperation in Nicolette's voice made her agree. "Yes, of course."

"Oh, bless you," Nicolette said, heaving a relieved breath through the phone. "Whenever you're ready, I can come pick you up. Or I can meet you there. Whatever you like. And no rush on time either. I know it's a Sunday and you probably—"

"Let's meet there," Amber said. "Just give me about half an hour to shower. I'll bring coffee and pastries."

Nicolette immediately began to cry. "Thank you, Amber," she choked out. "Mel was lucky to have you as a friend."

Willing back her own tears, she said, "I'll see you soon, okay?"

After a quick shower, Amber dressed, fed the cats, and hurried downstairs. She didn't open on Sundays until after ten, so she had plenty of time to help Nicolette and get back to the shop. To be on the safe side, she swiped a hand over her magicked blackboard to say, "Closed until noon!" The top-hat-wearing cat of her logo now tipped his hat, his fingers gripping the brim while he winked at his audience.

Locking up, she slipped out onto the deserted sidewalk of Russian Blue Avenue, walked around the building, and down the alley between her building and the next. The morning air was crisp and, given the occasional puddle she had to sidestep on the way to her car, it had rained last night. A fine mist hung in the air. Amber huddled a little more into her belted trench coat.

Amber stopped in at Purrcolate to grab coffees and Jack

Terrence's famous blueberry scones. His scones could uplift anyone's mood.

As she crossed the parking lot, she tried not to think about the last time she had been here. About hateful Susie Paulson vaguely accusing her of murder. About Whitney Sadler's expression and her tone turning cold as soon as Amber had mentioned Melanie's secret lover. About Kimberly telling Amber that Susie and Whitney had been in a heated conversation after the Here and Meow meeting.

Amber pushed open the door to the coffee shop and was immediately hit with the smell of baking scones. She exhaled deeply. A handful of people were already holed up at the small, sleek tables, laptops open next to coffee mugs and small plates dotted with crumbs. One couldn't resist the call of a Jack Terrence scone for long.

Both brothers were behind the counter, though Larry's attention was currently focused on a crossword puzzle. His arms were crossed on the black counter, his pen's cap wedged between his teeth as he stared at the half-filled-out puzzle.

Jack grinned and waved at her when she walked in. "Hi."

Amber smiled at him as she approached. Jack was a good-looking guy—smooth complexion with a smattering of freckles on his nose that he likely got from spending a good amount of time in the sun, short black hair, and green eyes. He always smiled like he'd been waiting all day to see her. He'd even asked her out once, but she'd turned him down.

Amber didn't date. At least, not non-witches. Not for a long time.

Jack was a sweetheart and needed someone who wasn't so

untrusting and guarded. In short, he needed someone who wasn't her.

"Hey, Jack," she said. "How are you?"

"Great, now that you're here."

"Ugh! *Boooo*," Larry called from the other end of the counter. Clearly, he had superhero hearing. He hadn't even looked up from his crossword puzzle. "That's the worst line I've ever heard! *Boooo*!"

Amber and Jack both laughed, but a healthy pink tint colored his cheeks. Jack threw a towel at his brother.

"You're the monster doing a crossword puzzle in *pen*," Jack said. "At least I'm not a psychopath."

"I prefer sociopath, thank you," Larry said, still not looking up from his puzzle. "I have a conscience."

"Clearly not!" said Jack. Then he turned his attention back to her. "So, what brings you in so early on a Sunday?"

She sighed. "I'm meeting up with Nicolette Cole in a few."

Jack's good humor deflated almost instantly. "Aw, man. The autopsy started, right?" When Amber nodded, he said, "I hope they find something to help them nail the bastard who did this."

"Me too."

"Whatever you want, it's on the house."

"Oh, you don't have to do that."

"No, I want to," Jack said. "Melanie gave us the Here and Meow job—it's going to be huge for us. She fought to get us approved even when that—"

"She-demon!" Larry supplied.

"—woman over at Clawsome Coffee raised a stink," Jack said. "Tell Nicolette it's from us."

Amber nodded. "Thanks. Just two coffees and two scones."

By the time Amber left with well wishes from both Jack and Larry, she was loaded down with a box of a dozen blueberry scones, as well as one of Jack's new raspberry creations, plus an iced coffee for Nicolette and a café mocha for herself.

Amber told herself she wasn't nervous about going to Melanie's house, but when she turned into Melanie's cul-de-sac and up to the small cottage-like house, the crumbs from two scones in her lap told her otherwise. She hardly remembered stress-eating her way through the pastries on the short drive over.

Nicolette's white, older-model Lexus was parked in the small driveway. Amber parked at the curb.

She climbed out of the car and brushed herself off. Then she tried to gracefully approach the waiting Nicolette—who stood outside her car, backside resting on her car door, staring off into space—while bundled down with two drinks, her purse, and a box of treats. When Nicolette saw her struggling, she hurried down the driveway to her.

"Oh, you're just so sweet for doing all this," Nicolette said, taking the box and her iced coffee, greedily sucking down half of it. "I needed this so bad. I'm running on fumes."

"No problem," Amber said. "The scones are courtesy of the Terrence brothers from Purrcolate."

Nicolette had already scarfed down part of one before Amber finished her sentence. "Holy hell, these are good."

They managed a bit of small talk in the driveway, standing

by Nicolette's car, before she let out a heaving sigh. "I suppose we should go in?"

Amber nodded. "Anything in particular you're looking for?"

"Pictures, maybe. Trinkets," Nicolette said, eyes welling with tears.

"We'll take it as slow as you need to, okay?" Amber said, giving the woman's arm a squeeze.

Nicolette nodded and sniffed hard. She straightened her shoulders, lifted her chin slightly, and then marched to her daughter's bright blue front door. The curtains, usually drawn open, were closed now. Amber was glad to see that yellow crime scene tape wasn't draped across the door in a giant X. She could almost convince herself that Melanie was on vacation and she and Nicolette had stopped by to water the houseplants Melanie didn't own.

Slipping the key into the lock, Nicolette looked over her shoulder at Amber.

"You got this," Amber said.

Nicolette nodded, let out a deep breath, and opened the door.

Amber stepped over the threshold after Nicolette, shoulders pulled up to her ears. Amber wasn't sure what she expected to find. The intruder lurking in the shadows with a syringe? Melanie's lingering ghost?

The house was eerily quiet. Especially since there were things shuffled around, making the house look more cluttered and messier than Melanie would have liked it. Drawers on side tables stood open. Cabinet doors stood ajar. Discarded items of clothing were draped over the back of the couch and heaped in a pile in the corner.

Amber wondered if the house had been like this when Melanie died, or if the police rooting around in the house had left it this way.

She shot a look at Nicolette, who stood in the middle of the living room, gaze darting across every inch of space. Yet she hadn't moved from the spot she'd stopped in, just past the little entryway, gripping her iced coffee with both hands.

"Why don't you go look in her room and see if there's anything in there you'd like to take with you?" Amber suggested.

Nicolette flinched slightly, her drink sloshing around violently for a moment, as if Amber had struck her. "Okay," she said softly, then moved across the hardwood floor toward the mouth of the hallway directly across from the front door. She turned right and disappeared.

Which left Amber alone in the living room—the room where Melanie had died. Amber took a slow drink of her coffee, hoping it would somehow soothe her.

Windows ran along the same wall as the front door, a large portion of them covered by an entertainment hutch. The giant dark wood piece housed a flat screen TV, while columns of storage space ran vertically on either side. A set of horizontal cabinets took up the space below it. The small doors were open, revealing a wide array of DVDs.

A two-seater loveseat rested against the wall across from the entertainment center, a coffee table between them. Amber placed the box of scones on the coffee table and tossed her purse onto the couch. Below the coffee table was a large throw rug covered in intricate designs of blue, red, and yellow. The oval coffee table was made of wood, its center glass. From Amber's snapshots of memory from Melanie, Amber knew that this rug was where her body had been dragged to and left after the killer had cleaned her up.

Amber wished she truly were a psychic, so she could touch the rug and ask it to tell its secrets, just as she had with Melanie's body. But while Melanie wasn't alive, she had been once. The same could not be said for the rug. She could likely use a spell to pull something from the fibers, as energy from high-emotion events often fused itself with an object at the moment of the trauma. The spells in her grimoire wouldn't be helpful, though, even if she had the time to sit here and work through the incantations.

Walking through the space between the coffee table and the couch, Amber moved away from the hallway where Nicolette had gone and toward the dining room. A large round table sat in the middle of the space. Amber had spent many evenings here, talking and laughing with Melanie about everything and nothing, drinking wine. Amber could almost hear Melanie calling her foul names as Amber won another hand of cards. Amber would laugh harder and harder as Melanie's colorful insults became increasingly creative the more she drank. On several occasions, a series of curses had gotten Amber and Melanie laughing so hard, they'd cried.

Amber bit her lip as she ran her fingertips over the worn wooden surface of the table.

Walking past the china cabinet that took up a large section of the side wall, Amber turned right into the kitchen. A place of hot chocolate, and frozen pizzas warming in the oven. The walls were yellow, the counters a soft gray granite. Cabinets and drawers, the wood dark and shiny, stood open here too. Amber slowly walked across the light gray tiles, methodically closing cabinets and rolling drawers back into place. A single white bowl and a mug with what looked like tea dregs at the bottom lay in the sink, a smudge of Melanie's red lipstick still marking the ceramic.

Amber heard Nicolette moving around in the one of the bedrooms and headed that way, the sight of the mug leaving Amber feeling exceedingly lonely for some reason. "Find anything?" she called out.

Nicolette didn't answer.

Amber passed the bathroom and then came to a stop in the middle of the hall, where Nicolette rummaged through Melanie's drawers, her back to Amber. Nicolette wasn't frantic, at least. Amber spotted Nicolette's empty iced coffee cup on the dresser and figured the woman was operating under caffeine power now.

The master bedroom was huge—easily half the size of Amber's entire studio apartment.

Amber's gaze landed on the set of windows at the back of the room, where the assailant had pried off a screen and entered with the intent to kill Melanie.

A low set of shelves ran under the windows. The room felt even more eerily quiet than the living room. This wasn't helped by the fact that the blinds Melanie had opened every day were closed. Light chased away—or revealed—things lingering in the shadows. She glanced over her shoulder at the bedroom door. Had the killer hidden behind it, waiting?

Amber shivered and grabbed the stick used to open the blinds. She gave it several twists, the blinds slowly opening and letting in the warm early morning sunlight.

A line of hedges ran around the outside of the house. They'd grown tall enough to obscure part of the view, but not enough to obscure the view of the man standing on the sidewalk, only a short stretch of lawn separating him from the house. He wore a tracksuit—dark blue or black—and had a baseball cap shielding the top part of his face. A white logo marked the hat, but she couldn't totally tell what it was from here. If she had to guess, she would have said it was an animal of some kind, its paw outstretched. Slowly, he raised a finger to his lips, as if to shush her. As if to tell her that his creeping outside was their little secret.

Amber gasped and stumbled back, hand to her chest.

Nicolette yelped from the other side of the room and whirled around, clearly not realizing Amber had even joined her. She dropped a jewelry box she'd been holding, which crashed to the hardwood floor. They both jumped. Rings and earrings and bracelets spilled across the floor. A hoop earring slid under the bed and bumped into the toe of Amber's shoe.

"What? What happened?" Nicolette said.

Amber was so shaken, it took her a moment to form a coherent thought. She looked to Nicolette and then back outside, finger pointing to the spot where she'd seen the man. The sidewalk was empty now. "There … there was a man."

"A man?" Nicolette said, rushing over to Amber's side of

the room. Amber flinched at the crunching sound of Melanie's spilled jewelry getting trampled underfoot. "What man?" she said, leaning against the set of drawers and peering outside, head swiveling left and right as if watching a tennis match.

"I don't know. He had a hat pulled down low. He was just standing there staring at the house. What the hell …"

Nicolette whirled to face her, jaw tight. Then, without warning, the woman ran out of the room.

Oh crap. Then Amber's mind caught up. She set down her coffee and dashed after her.

Nicolette ran down the hall, into the living room, yanked open the front door, and tore off down the driveway. She vanished around the side of the house before Amber had made it outside. Amber picked up the pace.

Melanie's house sat on the bottom of the U of her cul-de-sac. Directly next to her house was a bike and walking path that led to a large park in the middle of the subdivision. It wasn't uncommon for people to walk on the path that snaked around behind Melanie's house, as the path led to the park. Amber suspected that the man she'd seen was someone out for a morning jog. Perhaps he had only stopped to gawk at the house because he knew it was the site of a homicide, and then he had taken off when he'd realized he'd been caught snooping.

Amber couldn't explain that to Nicolette though, as the woman was hauling tail now, well behind the house and nearly sprinting down the sidewalk. By the time Amber reached her, the woman was standing at the entrance to the park. Only a woman pushing a stroller was here, near the empty jungle gym. The man, whoever he was, was long gone.

He had likely dived into someone's yard when he'd heard Nicolette tearing behind him like a mad woman.

"It could have been anyone," Amber said, heaving. She'd never been much of a runner. "C'mon, let's head back."

They walked slowly back to the house, not saying a word. The silence wasn't awkward, per se, but Amber got the impression Nicolette was a little embarrassed that she'd reacted so drastically.

When they got back to the house, Amber glanced down the driveway and immediately came up short. A white object rested on Nicolette's windshield. Amber walked to the car, eyeing the quiet street for any sign of movement. The object was a folded piece of paper resting under the windshield wiper.

"What's that?" Nicolette asked, coming to stand beside her, but then snatched it out of its resting place before Amber could reply. She grunted in disgust. "What's *wrong* with this town?" She thrust the note at Amber, then stalked back to the house.

Amber was almost too scared to unfold the note. Blowing out a breath, she opened it.

Written in blocky letters was: MELANIE DIDN'T BELONG HERE. WHEN SHE WOULDN'T LEAVE, I MADE SURE SHE STAYED GONE.

Nicolette couldn't concentrate after that. Amber, her nerves also frazzled, found her coffee, still sitting on Melanie's nightstand, and chugged down the contents. The pair locked up the house and parted ways. Nicolette, after much convincing, agreed to go back to her hotel with the box of scones. Amber assured her that she would report it all to the police, and pleaded with her to get some rest. The bags under Nicolette's eyes were even starker than the ones under the chief's.

The note burned a hole in Amber's pocket as she drove back to her shop, not the station. Was it *worth* taking to the chief? It was written in black ink on what looked like run-of-the-mill white computer paper. The note itself gave away nothing.

Perhaps it had been left by the man Amber had seen. Maybe it was someone else entirely. Maybe the guy had been out there as a distraction so Amber and Nicolette would be preoccupied while a second person placed the note on the car. But the lurker couldn't have known anyone would open the blinds and look out the back windows. Amber had chosen to do so on a whim.

Perhaps the note had been left on the car while Amber and Nicolette were inside, and by the time they came barreling out of the house, the note deliverer had come and gone. Maybe it had been there when they ran out and simply hadn't seen it. The man Amber had seen could have been nothing more than an innocent, if creepy, gawker.

Amber sat in her car, not sure if she should get out and go about her day as usual or pull back out of the lot and take the note to Chief Brown. Even if they had a tentative alliance now, willingly seeking him out was a foreign concept.

She couldn't get the image of the man on the sidewalk behind Melanie's house out of her head. The way he'd brought his finger to his lips. Shushing *her* when *he'd* been the one creeping about.

142

Pulling her phone out of her purse, she searched "roaring animal" logos. What came up was overwhelmingly skewed to sports teams. When she added "Edgehill" to the mix, the first hit was the town's little league team. Goose bumps broke out across her skin. It was a roaring tiger in all white, paw extended with its talons out. It was the same logo she'd seen on the man's hat.

What was a grown man doing wearing a hat for a little league team? A parent? A coach?

She looked up the team next. The site wasn't the best looking—stark red font on a gray background—but it was easy enough to navigate. She clicked on the staff page and nearly dropped her phone.

Under the label of coach was the smiling face of Derrick Sadler.

CHAPTER 11

After a bit more snooping, Amber figured out that the park where Derrick coached little league was only a mile from where Melanie lived. Had that been him outside? He'd had no reason to be there, had he? Certainly not standing outside, staring at the back of the house of his dead mistress. Especially not at the location where the assailant had snuck in so he could lie in wait for the unsuspecting Melanie.

With some maneuvering, she got the note out of her pocket while staying in the front seat of her car. She unfolded the paper with slightly shaking fingers.

MELANIE DIDN'T BELONG HERE. WHEN SHE WOULDN'T LEAVE, I MADE SURE SHE STAYED GONE.

Had Derrick been upset Melanie had followed him to Edge-hill? Had he broken up with her and she hadn't taken no for an answer? Had he killed her when he couldn't convince her he wasn't going to leave Whitney?

Chief Brown had said he didn't believe Derrick was dangerous, but if that had been him behind Melanie's house and the one who'd left the note, Amber wasn't sure the chief was right.

Amber needed to find out where he'd been this morning.

Unfortunately, there was only one person who she could

think of to ask, and she didn't know how much Whitney knew. Sure, the whole town seemed to be talking about Derrick's extramarital activities, but were people confronting Whitney about it at this point too? Amber didn't want to be the one to spill the beans.

So, instead, Amber called Kimberly Jones.

"Oh my God, Amber, hi!" Kim said. "This is so weird. I was just about to call you. Are you psychic or something?"

Depends on who you ask, she wanted to say. "Hardly," she said, laughing. "What's up?"

"It's kind of a sensitive subject. Can I come talk in person?"

Amber's stomach flipped. "Yeah, of course."

"Oh great," she said, heaving a sigh of relief. "I'm still upset about it. I'll be there in a jiff, okay?"

A jiff was just shy of ten minutes. Kimberly pulled into the parking lot behind Amber's building and hurriedly got out of the car. Her hair and makeup were done to perfection, as usual, even though it was barely eight-thirty.

Amber got out of her car when Kim did, but her greeting died on her lips. "Kim, what's wrong?"

Kimberly knocked back the fur-lined hood of her black jacket and sniffed. She ran her fingers through her long dark hair. Her eyes were red-rimmed.

"Have you been crying?" Amber asked, taking a few steps forward.

Kimberly's eyes welled up, then her gaze darted back and forth across the small lot behind the building. Their cars were the only ones there, and on the other end, a pair of cats prowled around a green dumpster.

"Can we talk inside?" she asked.

The two headed up to Amber's apartment, Kimberly sniffling with every step across the wood floors of the Quirky Whisker and up each stair leading to the studio above. It wasn't until Kim was in the apartment that Amber realized Kim had never been here. They hadn't hung out much since high school.

"Oh my God, Amber," she managed, giving the room a scan as she turned in a slow circle, still sniffing periodically. "Your place is adorable!"

Alley came trotting out at the sound of a female voice. Tom watched warily from under the bed, his nose poking out from behind the dust ruffle. Kim scooped Alley into her arms, the cat purring so loud, Amber could hear it from several feet away. Kim buried her face in Alley's fur. Alley's eyes squinted shut in delight.

"That cat hardly tolerates me, let alone strangers," said Amber, eyeing her cat as she nuzzled her head against Kim's chest and closed her eyes.

"I've been told I'm a bit of a cat whisperer." She carefully made her way to the couch and sat without upsetting Alley too much. The undivided feline attention seemed to have helped bring her emotions under control. The sniffing stopped.

Amber plopped down next to her on her tiny couch, self-conscious suddenly of the mess of plastic bits scattered across her coffee table. Then Amber noticed her stack of papers littered with half-formed spells.

Crap.

Thankfully, Kim was so preoccupied with Alley and her

ridiculous display of joy that Amber was able to discreetly slip the sheets of papers under an innocuous celebrity gossip magazine.

"So what did you want to talk to me about?" Amber asked, voice soft, much like the tone she often used to coax scaredy-cat Tom out from under the bed.

"Oh …" Kim said, gaze focused on the black-and-white cat who was now curled in a ball in her lap. Kim scritched behind Alley's left ear. "Whitney Sadler called me this morning."

"What? *Why*?" Amber asked, loud enough that it startled Alley, who abruptly sprang from Kim's lap and darted under the bed with Tom, the dust ruffle swishing back into place after her.

Kim stared in that direction, bottom lip partially stuck out. She looked as if she might start crying again.

"Sorry," Amber said, blowing out a slow breath, realizing how ridiculous her little outburst had been. Kim was now the head chair for the Here and Meow, and Whitney was in charge of finances. The two would likely be in conversation often now that Melanie was gone. "Is Whitney responsible for …" Amber vaguely gestured in Kim's general direction.

With a nod, she turned to face Amber, one leg propped up on the couch cushion. "She found out about the affair."

Amber winced. "Who told her?"

"Oh, lord knows at this point," Kimberly said. "But I think she found out today. Henrietta Bishop lives across the street from them and she was drinking her morning coffee on her porch and saw the whole thing."

Amber wondered if Henrietta Bishop still thought Amber

should market her sleepy tea, given the events of late. Amber pictured her standing on her porch, slowly sipping her coffee, her mane of red hair spilling down her back as she watched the family drama play out before her across the street.

Amber often mentally chastised the people of Edgehill on the whole for being so caught up in gossip. There was a difference between being a concerned neighbor and being a busybody.

But she would be lying if she said she wasn't just as easily ensnared by it all. "*What* whole thing?"

"Okay, so Derrick apparently goes for a run like clockwork from seven-thirty to eight-thirty," Kimberly said. "Around eight, Henrietta is sitting on her porch minding her own business, and next thing she knows, Whitney's door opens and Whitney storms out in a rage, holding an armful of clothes. She tosses it onto the lawn. Then stomps back and in and comes out with more. Suits and ties and shoes—all of it on the lawn. She threw out books, sports equipment, even electronics."

"Geez!"

"I know!" said Kim, no sign of tears now, wrapped up as she was in her story, sitting cross-legged on the couch. "She's still at it when Derrick comes home from his run and he starts screaming at her, asking what the heck she's doing. Whitney starts screaming back. Saying stuff like, 'How long was it going on this time?' and 'Do vows mean nothing to you?' and …"

Amber tried to wait her out but caved almost immediately. "And?"

"And she asked, 'Did *you* kill her?'"

Amber gasped. "She accused him out in the open like that?"

148

"Oh yeah," she said. "Henrietta said Whitney came running down the porch steps and started pounding on his chest, screaming, 'Did you kill Melanie? Did you? Are you a cheat *and* a murderer?'"

Amber's eyes were so wide, it was a wonder they didn't fall out of her head. "What did Derrick say?"

"Henrietta said Derrick kept saying, 'Of course not!' and 'How could you even ask that?' and Whitney was sobbing and kicking at the huge pile of stuff on the lawn and he was trying to get her to calm down because obviously *everyone* was peeking out windows and doors by this point," Kim said. "He was trying to pull her to him to hug her, I guess, but to also get her in the house. She shoved him away, ran inside, locked the door, and wouldn't let him in.

"She must have barricaded the door or something because even though he had a key, he couldn't get in. Henrietta said it looked that way anyway.

"Eventually he gave up and stormed down the sidewalk. He caught Henrietta staring at him as he went by her house and he said, 'Enjoying the show?'"

Amber winced.

"I know."

"Where did he go?"

"Heck if I know."

Amber heaved out a sigh. "Wait … you said Whitney called *you*? How does that fit in?"

Kimberly groaned and tipped her head back to stare at the ceiling. Thankfully, when she lowered her face to look at

Amber again, her eyes were dry. "She called me and asked if it was true that I'd caught them together."

"No!" Amber said. "Who told her *that*?"

"I don't know," Kim said, shaking her head. "You're the only one I told, and I doubt you've been chatting it up with Whitney."

Not yet, anyway. "Wasn't me."

With a nod, Kimberly said, "She kept pushing me until I admitted that I knew. Then she started calling me a horrible friend—ha, like I was ever friends with Whitney-freaking-Sadler—for never telling her. Asked how I slept at night knowing about this for months. Asked how I could sit across from her during committee meetings with her *and* Melanie and act like everything was fine when I knew Melanie was—" Kim pursed her lips. "She used a nasty word here I'm not going to repeat, but it rhymes with a water bird. She wanted to know how I never told her Melanie was ... birding her husband."

"What did you say?"

"That Melanie asked me not to," Kimberly said. "It sounds so stupid now! If I'd known what would happen to Melanie, I would have screamed about the affair from the rooftops."

"She should be upset with her husband, not with you," Amber said.

"Oh, she's plenty ticked at Derrick," Kimberly said. "Just before she hung up, she was like, 'Well, I hope Melanie knows she got her wish. I'm filing for divorce. She can have him.' Then she hung up."

A swirling ball of rage writhed in Amber's gut. "Melanie is *dead*. How could she say something like that?"

Kimberly shook her head. "She's hurting. She'll regret saying that once emotions aren't so high."

It didn't stop Amber from wanting to clock Whitney.

"She also said she quits as finance chair for the Here and Meow," Kim said. "She's been running that side of things for five years. Finding her replacement will be a nightmare."

As it fell silent, the events of Amber's own morning caught back up with her. "I think I had a run-in with Derrick Sadler just before all this happened."

"Wait, what?" Kim asked.

Amber told her about the whole saga of the morning—everything from Nicolette's early morning phone call to the creeper Amber and Nicolette had chased down. Kim had listened, eyes wide, as she clutched a throw pillow to her chest.

"Oh my God, Amber! You really think it was Derrick?"

"Can't be sure, but the timing lines up. The guy was in a tracksuit and baseball cap. He lives about a mile from Melanie's place. If he runs every day, the mile from his house to hers would be nothing for him."

"But why would he be outside her house?" Kim asked. Then she sighed, hand to her throat. "What if he's so heartbroken that he runs there on auto-pilot—like he can't stay away even though she's gone?"

Amber recalled the way he'd brought a finger to his lips, shushing her. "Or returning to the scene of the crime …"

"You don't really think he did it, do you?" Kim asked. "I mean, I know he wasn't rushing to leave Whitney for her or anything, but he loved Mel. I could tell."

Amber sighed. She really didn't know what to think anymore.

Amber wondered which version of Derrick was the true one. The cheating, conniving man Whitney thought he was, or the lovesick one Kimberly pegged him to be. Then, of course, there was whatever version Melanie had known and loved.

"Did Derrick ever talk to you about catching them?" Amber suddenly asked. "Did he ask you not to say anything about it? Confront you in any way?"

"No more than you'd expect in that kind of situation, I guess?"

Brow furrowed, Amber said, "What do you mean?"

"Well, like, after I caught them, and I had that long chat with Melanie, Derrick and I ran into each other at the grocery store the next day and he said he'd appreciate it if I didn't say anything to anyone about what I saw," she said. "I said of course I wouldn't. He sent thank-you flowers to my work a week later with a gift card to that really fancy day spa in Belhaven. He sent flowers once every couple months." Kim wrinkled her nose. "Now that I think about it, I ran into him quite a few times in town after I caught them. The post office, a restaurant, a couple of coffee shops …"

Amber's mouth bunched up on one side. "Did that make you uncomfortable?"

Kim cocked her head. "What part?"

"Any of it?"

Kim shrugged. "Running into people in town here is pretty common, so that wasn't too weird. Though I haven't seen him much since then. And the gifts ..." She shrugged again. "He was just thanking me."

"It didn't seem like he was bribing you to keep quiet?" Amber asked.

She pursed her lips. "Well, it sounds bad now that you word it that way."

"Did he ever follow you or threaten you? Anything like that?"

"Nope, just the presents," she said. "I took it as a sign that he really wanted to keep Melanie safe, you know? He was looking out for her because he knew how bad things could get for her—for them both—if word got out."

"Bad enough that someone would kill her over it?" Amber asked.

Kim's eyes welled up and she clutched the pillow a little tighter.

"Sorry," Amber said. In a softer tone, she said, "You don't think it was Derrick."

Kimberly wrinkled her nose and shook her head.

"Who do you think it was?"

A pink hue slowly crept into Kimberly's cheeks and she kept her gaze focused on her legs, which were still crossed on the couch cushions.

"What?" Amber asked. When Kim wouldn't reply, Amber attempted to lighten the mood. "Oh no. Do you think it was *me*?"

Kim's head snapped up. "No! Of course not. I just ... I don't like to throw blame around. But ..."

Amber waited her out this time.

"Okay, so Ann Marie and I were eating dinner last night and she told me about this really weird thing that happened yesterday. She went into Paws 4 Tea to get something for her mom's birthday and Susie was working. Ann Marie only started this year as Susie's assistant for volunteer services or whatever, but the two have worked together enough by now that Ann Marie would call Susie an acquaintance, at least. But, I mean, you know Susie. She's not the easiest person to deal with. She's not super friendly *or* chatty and Ann Marie can be a total chatterbox, so working with Susie has been a bit hard on her.

"Anyway, she said Susie was *super* chatty when Ann Marie went in yesterday. Susie was asking if Ann Marie had heard anything about an official vote to assign *my* assistant. She was pitching herself to Ann Marie as if Ann Marie was holding an interview or something!"

"How odd," Amber said.

"Right?" asked Kimberly. "But, I mean, you know Susie's been gunning for the lead festival director job for, like, ever, right? She's always outvoted."

"It would help if she didn't have the personality of a snapping turtle."

Kim let out a shocked bark of laughter, then covered her mouth. When her giggling subsided, she said, "If Susie wants to be my assistant, why she doesn't come to *me*?"

Amber shrugged. "I'm sure some part of her is upset she got passed up for the position twice this year now. Outvoted two times in a few months has to sting. Her ego is almost as big as her head."

Kim erupted in giggles again. "Oh my God, Amber, you're awful!"

Amber truly didn't like Susie Paulson, but she was putting more effort into it now, to keep Kimberly laughing. "She probably holds some animosity toward you for getting the position even though the choice obviously wasn't yours," Amber said. "But if she truly wants to work with you, she'll have to get over that."

Kimberly mulled that over. Given her slight frown, it was clear she didn't like the idea of working with Susie Paulson. "I'm not saying I think Susie would kill Melanie to become the head of the Here and Meow Committee, because that would be insane. But, oh, I don't know … I just remember how royally pissed she was when Melanie was voted in. She cursed up a storm and then slammed her way out of the town hall meeting."

Amber remembered that, too.

But as much as she disliked Susie, she thought resorting to murder to get what she wanted was a bit of a stretch. Even for her.

At least she hoped it was.

The two women chatted for a little while longer, then Kimberly said she had to get going. She was meeting with Ann Marie and Nathan to work on finding a new finance chair.

Amber walked Kimberly out and hugged her goodbye. As she watched the woman round the side of the Quirky Whisker and disappear between her building and the next, Amber's mind flitted back to Whitney.

Amber had been so sure that Whitney had known about

the affair. The abrupt way Whitney had cut her off during their conversation outside Purrcolate, at the very least, showed Whitney knew something about Melanie's entanglement with the "mystery man," whether or not she knew that man had been her own husband.

Whitney had known *something*.

And Amber was determined to figure out just what that was.

CHAPTER 12

Amber checked that her magicked blackboard showed her return time was still noon—sometimes if she was in too much of a hurry when altering the spell on the board, the magic would glitch. She'd once hastily crafted a spell on the board that, upon her return, had listed her return time as thirty-seven o'clock, and her top-hat-wearing logo had looked as if someone had spiked his milk with aged rum.

Satisfied that her cat logo looked to be in perfect health, Amber locked up her shop and walked across Russian Blue Avenue to Purrfectly Scrumptious. Savannah lounged in the wicker cat bed by the door. She was too busy dozing to acknowledge Amber.

The small shop was always immaculate and gleaming, and, just like always, smelled of sugar and vanilla. The floors were shiny white tile, the countertops a pink granite. Cabinets, light fixtures, and even the trim around the doors and windows were a light pink. In most circumstances, Amber would have thought the color scheme to be garish, but somehow Betty had made it homey, rather than resembling the scene of a cotton candy explosion.

Betty was behind the counter to her right, head down as she focused on getting the swirl of white frosting out of her piping bag and onto the chocolate cupcakes waiting patiently before her in two neat rows of six each. Large, curving glass-enclosed cases displaying her treats sat on either side, partially blocking Betty's view of the door.

Directly across from the front door was the swinging door that led to the back of the shop, where the bigger ovens and supplies were stored. The door opened and an elderly, tall African-American man with a smear of flour across his forehead poked his head out.

"Oh hi, Amber," he said, walking out into the shop. "I thought I heard someone come in. You know Betty is deaf to the world when she's frosting." He said this as he wiped his hands on his flour-coated apron, hand outstretched as he headed toward her.

Amber grinned. "Hi, Bobby." She shook his hand as if she hadn't known Betty's husband her entire life. But shaking hands in greeting was Bobby's way, whether you hadn't seen him in years, or just yesterday.

Betty looked up then, eyes slightly glazed over, as if coming out of a daze. "Hey, honey," she said to Amber.

"Hey, Betty."

"How you doing? People treating you okay?" Bobby asked, hands on hips, as if he planned on roughing up anyone who might be giving her a hard time. Amber figured Betty had filled him in on the details.

"They are now … at least now that they know I don't go around poisoning people," Amber said.

"Pah! Forget the lot of 'em," Bobby said, swiping at the

air in frustration. Then he jutted a chin at her. "How's that sister of yours?"

They fell into amicable small talk for a while, allowing Betty to finish up with her cupcakes. Out of the corner of her eye, Amber saw that Betty adorned each cupcake with a set of intricately designed black-and-gray candy cat ears.

When Betty was done, she came around the side of one of the glass display cases and playfully swatted Bobby on the butt with the towel she'd used to wipe her hands of frosting. "You get back to baking, Bobby! Stop asking so many questions; leave the poor girl alone."

Bobby had been perfectly lovely, as always. He grinned at Amber and waved, taking several backward steps. "Can't argue with the missus. See you around! Don't let any of the knuckleheads out there—" he gestured back and forth with a finger aimed at Russian Blue Avenue behind her "—get into your head, you hear me?"

Amber nodded. "Good talking to you, Bobby."

"You too, honey, you too." He was almost to the back door when he suddenly darted forward again, wrapped a hand around either of Betty's shoulders, and placed a loud kiss on her cheek.

Betty laughed, swatting him away. Bobby winked at Amber, then disappeared into the back of the shop. Betty was shaking her head and clucking her tongue, but Amber didn't miss the smile playing at the woman's mouth. She gave her head a little shake, trying to refocus. "What can I help you with, sugar?"

"I don't suppose you heard the latest about the Sadlers?"

Betty's brows arched. "I've been here all morning …"

Amber caught Betty up to speed, feeling a little smug that it was finally Amber who had town gossip before the infamous Betty Harris did.

When Amber got to the end of her story, Betty clucked her tongue, shaking her head again. "Poor Whitney ..."

"I know. So ... I was thinking I could grab some sympathy cupcakes and then go see how she's doing?"

Amber didn't want Betty to know that these were actually bribery cupcakes, used to pull information out of someone in crisis. Betty thought so highly of Amber and Amber didn't want to sully the woman's impression of her with something as unimportant as the truth.

"That's a really nice idea," Betty said, already heading behind the counter again. "I suggest Chocolate Chocolate Surprise—the surprise is more chocolate—and Coconut Cream Delight."

Amber's mouth watered at the name of the second. Betty's coconut cream cupcakes were the stuff of legend. "I'll take three of each."

Amber watched Betty for a moment as she carefully selected cupcakes from within the glass display cases and placed them in an awaiting pink box. Amber's second box of treats for the day and it wasn't even noon yet!

"I should thank you, by the way," she said.

"What for?" Betty asked, gaze concentrated on getting the last cupcake into the plastic partition at the bottom of the box.

"A big reason why Chief Brown no longer has me at the top of his suspect list is because you supplied my alibi," Amber said. "He knows I was in my shop at the time of Melanie's death because you were across the street and saw me."

Once she got the box with the plastic window on top securely closed, Betty walked back to where Amber waited. "Even if I hadn't seen you for a week, I'd still tell him you were a good egg and I didn't think for a second you'd hurt a fly." She handed the pink box over.

It was heavy in her hands. Given the two scones she'd scarfed down earlier, she really shouldn't eat anything else laden with sugar today—at least not until she had a proper breakfast—but lord help her, did she ever want to shove every last one of the cupcakes in her mouth. She looked up at Betty and smiled. "Thank you. For everything."

Betty softly clucked her tongue and affectionately patted Amber's cheek. "Nothing to thank me for, sugar." She took a step back and jutted her chin at the box, a gesture that looked identical to the one Bobby had used earlier. "And those are on the house."

"Betty …"

"Nope!" she said, hand in the air. "I don't want to hear it. Now get on out of here and make sure Mrs. Sadler's okay."

As Amber walked to her car, she hoped Whitney would talk to her.

No one in their right mind turned down cupcakes, did they?

Amber idled at the curb, the intersection of Puma Way and American Curl Avenue a few feet away. The Sadlers lived on

American Curl. She hadn't known that until today; it was amazing what information was floating around online for nosy women to find when they needed to drop in on someone grieving the end of their marriage. Amber had added a few drops of a calming tincture to both a Chocolate Chocolate Surprise and a Coconut Cream Delight, hoping that once Whitney bit into one of the cupcakes, her emotional state would be knocked down a peg. Amber really didn't want assorted electronics thrown at her head.

Amber glanced at the map lying on top of the cupcake box in the passenger seat. Once the internet had granted her the information she needed about which house belonged to the Sadlers, Amber had gone to a convenience store down the street from the Quirky Whisker and purchased a map of Edgehill. Then, once safely locked inside her studio apartment, she'd laid out the map on her dining room table, gotten out her crystals and grimoire, and pulled up a picture of Whitney Sadler on her computer.

Locator spells could be tricky, as the witch's intent for finding the object or person in question was sometimes hindered by the object or person's desire to be found. This was made more difficult when Amber didn't have something belonging to Whitney while scrying. Amber had to hope that a picture of her would be enough, but she was well aware that it could potentially not work at all.

After several tries and tweaking the wording of her spell, all while holding her amethyst crystal—used to help strengthen her magic ... often with mixed results—a dot had sprung up on the map, right in the location that Google had told her the

Sadlers lived. Amber watched as the dot moved periodically, but not more than a couple millimeters in either direction.

Whitney Sadler was home.

And, according to the map lying on top of the cupcake box, Whitney was *still* home.

Amber just needed to get herself around the corner of American Curl Avenue, park in front of the Sadler house, and present Whitney with her tincture-laden cupcakes. Amber told herself she was doing this all for Melanie.

A voice that sounded suspiciously like Chief Brown's rumbled in the back of her mind. A voice telling her that she wasn't supposed to be "harassing" potential witnesses connected to the case without talking to him first. But she wasn't *harassing* Whitney. She was being a friend. A well-meaning acquaintance? Okay, perhaps well-meaning was a stretch, too.

She told the voice in her head to put a sock in it.

Blowing out a deep breath and giving the map another quick glance to make sure the black dot representing Whitney Sadler was still where she needed it to be, Amber put her car in drive and turned onto American Curl.

This block—as well the blocks surrounding it in either direction—made up the ritzier part of town. Houses here boasted large front lawns that were set back from the sidewalk. Most had large, leafy trees in their yards, providing abundant shade in the summer. This was one of the picturesque streets that the Here and Meow 5k went past, giving the runners a glimpse at how the well-to-do in Edgehill lived.

Whitney Sadler's house was on the right, about halfway down the block. The house was two-storied, painted a rich blue, and had white trim. Six steps led up to the porch, large bay windows looking out on the street. White pillars sat on either side of the staircase.

There were still signs of Whitney's earlier tirade on the lawn. A white dress shirt atop the low hedge that ran around the house. A single black loafer overturned on the grass. A deep-green tie lying across the cement walkway that led to the porch's steps, looking more like a slithering snake than a discarded accessory.

Amber parked at the curb, fished the pink box out of the passenger seat, and then walked cautiously up the front walk. She wondered if Henrietta was watching this from the safety of her own home across the street.

Just seconds from knocking, the front door was wrenched open. Amber startled. Whitney peered out, eyes squinted. Her eyes were red and her hair was loose around her shoulders, rather than in its usual tight ponytail. It made her look younger somehow.

"What do you want, Amber?" Whitney asked, arms crossed. She stood in the open doorway of her house as if she were a bouncer checking IDs outside a club.

Amber flipped open the lid of the box and held the cupcakes out as an offering.

Whitney craned her neck ever so slightly to get a better view of the treats. "I'll make coffee." Then she turned on her heel and disappeared into the house, leaving Amber on the porch.

Amber let herself in and closed the door behind her.

The Sadler house, much like the series of pictures Amber

had seen in Whitney's social media feed, looked like it belonged in a magazine. The floors were made of a dark wood, and the staircase across from her that led to the second story was painted a bright eggshell white.

In the entrance of the house was a small seating area. Elegant throw pillows adorned with tassels or hanging gems at the corners sat positioned *just so* on the cushions of two pristine cream-and-baby-blue chairs that sat on one side of a gray leather ottoman. A plush-looking white shaggy rug sat beneath it. On the other side was a white leather couch, a gray cashmere blanket folded and draped over the back. A fireplace with a row of delicate blue vases lining the mantle took up part of the wall to Amber's left.

Amber wondered how on earth Whitney kept the place so clean, and assumed she couldn't possibly have pets. But a second later, a pair of fluffy gray kittens came barreling down the steps, nearly slid into the wall in their haste, and darted into the room to the right of the front door, which was marked by a set of open pocket doors. A large wooden dining table took up most of the space. Amber deposited the cake box onto it.

What sounded like a coffee grinder whirred to life, and Amber followed the noise and the scampering kittens into the kitchen, where Whitney was busy preparing coffee. Amber stood awkwardly in the open doorway, wondering if she should be helping. After a minute, Whitney wordlessly pulled open a cabinet and drawer, handing Amber a pair of cake plates and forks.

Amber assumed they were for the cupcakes and took them, situating herself in the magazine set of a dining room. A white china cabinet ran along the wall opposite where Amber waited in a high-backed chair. A marble bust of a man with high cheekbones sat atop the cabinet, watching Amber with flat eyes and a mildly disapproving stare.

Ignoring him, Amber placed a Chocolate Chocolate Surprise cupcake—the one with the calming tincture added to the frosting—on Whitney's plate, and grabbed a Coconut Cream Delight for herself. Amber stared at the set of forks Whitney had given her. Did rich folks eat cupcakes with forks? Amber found this notion even more monstrous than Larry Terrence doing a crossword puzzle with ink.

Coffee was brought to the table and Amber picked at her cupcake and Whitney shoveled mouthfuls of chocolate cupcake into her mouth. No one spoke. The only sounds were of utensils clicking against plates and the bounding, thunderous feet of tiny kitten paws as the pair raced across the wood floors. The silence was driving Amber batty, but she needed to give her calming tincture time to work.

Besides, now that she was here, her anger at Whitney had mostly dried up. She just felt sorry for her now. The woman reminded Amber of something porcelain and delicate—one little nudge toward the edge she balanced on precariously, and she'd fall and break.

The minutes ticked by. Despite Betty's coconut cupcakes being Amber's favorite treat in the world, she couldn't get herself to eat more than a few tiny forkfuls. Her stomach was sick, her palms were sweating, and Amber truly wasn't altogether sure what to make of her emotions.

Suddenly, Whitney let out a long groan and slouched back

in her chair. "Wow, that really hit the spot. Sometimes a girl just needs a little chocolate, you know?"

Amber nodded. "I was hoping it would help."

"It was perfect," Whitney said, hand on her stomach like she'd just won a pie-eating contest, not that she'd eaten a single cupcake.

Amber only let the silence linger for another moment before she said, "I ... uh ... I heard about what happened with Derrick. I'm really sorry."

"Bah!" Whitney said, sticking out her tongue just slightly. "He's an idiot." Then she squinted at Amber. In a calm tone, like she was discussing something as asinine as the weather, she asked, "Did you know, too? Melanie, that little hussy friend of yours, was your best bud, wasn't she? Did the two of you talk about what a great lay my husband is? Did she give you every scintillating detail?"

Amber was torn between being pissed off, horrified, and ashamed. Heat flooded her cheeks. "Don't call her that. And, *no*, I didn't know. Not until after ... until she was ..."

"Dead," Whitney said, reaching forward with a manicured finger to dab at a chocolate crumb resting on the edge of her white cake plate, then bringing it to her mouth. The chocolate-covered cupcake wrapper lay folded in a neat triangle.

Amber clenched her jaw. "Melanie and Derrick had met before Edgehill, hadn't they?"

Whitney, still slouched a bit in her high-backed chair—Amber had never seen Whitney slouch—scooted back a little and rested an elbow on the armrest, her chin propped up on her fist. "Why do you care?"

It wasn't said with malice. Just curiosity. Calm for Whitney Sadler apparently meant the lack of a mental filter.

Amber considered how best to answer the question. She needed Whitney to confide in her, and Amber would likely only have the opportunity while Whitney's guard was down. So she went with what Whitney would want to hear, while also sticking to the truth. "Because I want to know what happened to my friend, but the more I learn about her, the more I realize I didn't truly know her. I feel a little duped."

"Ha!" Whitney said, sitting straighter. "*You* feel duped. Imagine how I feel." She ran a hand through her loose blonde hair. "They met at a work conference."

Just like Nicolette had said.

"It was some tech conference, I think? I don't know. Derrick jets off to those things all the time. He's a wizard with numbers and has a head for business, so he goes to these things to network and make business connections."

"Melanie was working for Northwind Consultants then, right?" Amber asked.

Whitney nodded. "They got to talking, one thing led to another ..."

Abruptly, Whitney got up from the table and headed into the kitchen. She returned a few seconds later, her hand wrapped around the neck of a bottle filled with an amber-colored liquid. She dumped a generous amount into her coffee, then held the bottle in Amber's direction, brows raised. Amber waved her off. With a shrug, Whitney set the bottle back down with a muted thud and plopped back into her seat.

She took a swig of her spiked coffee, winced, then took

another sip. She sat back, slouched again. "When he got back from the trip, he broke down crying. He said he was sorry and it would never happen again. Blah blah. I was six months pregnant with Sydney. I'd dropped out of med school by then. We said I'd go back after the baby was born. I think he knew there was nowhere for me to go. I couldn't raise a baby on my own and my parents are a nightmare." She laughed, but there was no humor in it.

"Did you know who Melanie was then?" Amber asked. "Or just that the affair happened?"

Whitney snatched up her coffee cup, then slowly drained the contents. "I went through his phone and his email one day while he was taking a nap. I was pregnant and hormonal and *pissed*. I found out who she was and stalked her. But ... and, God, I'm so stupid, but Derrick was such an angel after that. He pampered me like I was a queen. Breakfast in bed, bought me random gifts, gave my disgusting swollen feet massages until I fell asleep. I really believed him when he said it was an accident and the result of too much drinking."

Amber pursed her lips but didn't say anything.

"So I forgot all about Melanie Cole and I had Sydney and she was the best thing that's ever happened to us. Derrick *adores* her." Whitney's dainty nostrils flared. "Then, almost two years ago, Melanie showed up in Edgehill. I spotted her at the Here and Meow—talking to *you*, of all people."

The day Amber had met Melanie.

"I didn't confront her. I mean, she had no idea who I was, as far I knew," Whitney said. "Derrick and I got into a blow-out fight that day. He swore he hadn't been seeing or talking to her. Had no idea what she was doing in Edgehill. It must have just been a coincidence."

"Did you believe him?"

Whitney rubbed her fingers back and forth across her forehead as if she was trying to rid herself of a headache. "Stupidly, yes. I ran into Melanie in town a couple times and she was always very polite. Recognition never dawned on her face, even when I mentioned Derrick was my husband. They barely acknowledged each other in public." She sighed. "I even asked Derrick to put one of those tracking apps on his phone, you know? As proof that he wasn't anywhere he wasn't supposed to be."

"Did he do it?"

"Willingly," Whitney said, nodding. "I truly thought this was all behind us. And then … then Melanie turns up dead and people are looking at me like *I've* done something. Then I find out that everyone in this damn town knew that my perfect husband was screwing Melanie—again—and no one had the decency to tell me." Her eyes rimmed with tears. "Everyone just whispered about it behind my back. I figure no one would have ever told me had Melanie not died."

Amber's stomach twisted. She figured Whitney was right. "What are you going to do now?"

Whitney let out a long, gusting sigh. "I have a brother on the East Coast. I may go see him for a while. I don't know about long term. I haven't worked in over ten years. God, I guess I need to dust off my résumé …"

Amber winced. She wasn't sure what she'd wanted to accomplish with this little visit, but feeling this level of sympathy for this porcelain doll of a woman hadn't been it. She hadn't anticipated wanting to track down Derrick simply so she could punch him in the face. He'd ruined Whitney's life and had possibly stolen Melanie's.

A phone rang in the kitchen.

Whitney groaned.

"I should probably go," Amber said, suddenly desperate to leave, and got to her feet. "I just wanted to check on you."

In a move that clearly surprised them both, Whitney rounded the table and pulled Amber into a hug. "Thank you," she said. "No one else has."

The phone stopped ringing, then immediately started again.

Amber let herself out of the house, leaving Whitney to answer the phone. She hoped it wasn't bad news. She wasn't sure how much more Whitney could take.

As Amber walked down the walkway to her car, she thought about that meeting she had with Derrick on Wednesday. That bubbling ball of rage simmered in her stomach again. She pulled out her cell.

She'd just sat down and closed herself in her car when the deep voice of Owen Brown said, "What can I do for you, Miss Blackwood?"

"So, about this wire …"

171

CHAPTER 13

Instead of dwelling on the very real possibility that she would be meeting with a killer on Wednesday, Amber spent a good deal of her Monday lost in the task of working on her peacock toy for Sydney Sadler. The action of the tail fanning out still gave her the most trouble.

To animate a toy, Amber had to infuse a small object with a spell that she then embedded into a section of her plastic creation. The more actions she needed to assign a certain part, the more complicated things became, as she required multiple spells to work in tandem. If she wanted the small magic-infused object to be the heart of multiple actions, she needed multiple spells layered in one location. If the spells in question weren't crafted perfectly, the magic in one location might act against another, causing the toy to malfunction.

Tiny plastic discs worked the best, and she'd inserted one in the tip of each tail feather. The feathers needed to close like a retractable fan—something the bird could drag behind it as it walked—but they also needed to spread out on command and then stay stationary while the bird strutted. For some reason, the spell-infused plastic discs malfunctioned in the steps between lifting the tail and fanning it out.

But on Tuesday evening, positioned on the floor before

her covered coffee table, the peacock effortlessly lifted its tail and spread it out to reveal the riot of color—bright blues and vibrant greens and hints of deep purple. The peacock shook its tail a bit, all with a smirk on its little beaked face and a twinkle in its tiny plastic black eye. Amber let out a yelp of triumph, fist in the air.

She watched the bird for a while as it strutted around like a model on a runway; Amber felt quite pleased with herself. Alley sat nearby and hissed where appropriate—mostly when the bird sauntered toward the edge of the coffee table before it turned around to strut in the other direction. Alley didn't fear the toys so much as distrust them. The hiss was to let it know she wasn't interested in being friends. Tom outright hated them and currently hid under the bed. That was how Amber knew the toy was done.

Now she just needed to layer one final spell on top of the peacock as a whole, one that would be triggered by Derrick Sadler's touch. A spell that would force him to give an honest answer to the question she last asked. Something more complicated and nuanced than the simple truth spell she'd used on Chief Brown.

Could she outright ask him if he'd killed Melanie? What would she do if he said yes? Would he retaliate if forced to confess?

She hoped if that happened, Chief Brown would get to her before Derrick hurt Amber, too.

On Wednesday, just before 11:00 a.m., Amber parked a few blocks away from Chartreux Way, one of the main streets in Edgehill, then walked into the Edgehill police station. She spotted Carl almost immediately. He had been chatting with the sour-faced receptionist, arms draped on the counter, one foot crossed over the other. The receptionist looked four hundred kinds of uninterested in whatever he was telling her. Luckily for Sour Face, he turned toward Amber when she walked in, a bright smile lighting up his features, his braces on full display.

"Come on back, Miss Blackwood!" Carl said, enthusiastically waving an arm. "The chief has all your stuff set up in here."

Carl led her to one of the larger interrogation rooms—at least that's what she thought this room was. It had a beige-topped table in the center, the corner nearest her cracked and showing thick brown material underneath. A pair of gray plastic chairs sat on either side of the table, and a large two-way mirror took up most of one wall.

The chief offered her only a nod in greeting. It was just as well; Amber only had eyes for what lay on the table. There were three walkie-talkie looking things, a black box with a wire snaking out of it and coming to a head at what looked like a tiny microphone, and an open laptop. The screen was black save for a series of long green hashes that were as long as five inches in places. Carl cleared his throat, and, on the right of the screen, Amber saw a spike in the green lines.

The chief picked up the small black box and held it in her direction. "This isn't the most high-tech of equipment, but it'll do for now. You'll attach this part to your pants at your waistline, and the wire will snake under your shirt. This part here …" He tapped the top of the little microphone head, and the green lines on the laptop screen jumped again. "This part will need to face out. It's sensitive, so if it slips under your clothes, all we'll hear is your movement."

"Like a butt dial," Carl offered.

The chief sighed. "Like a butt dial."

Carl nodded sagely, brows pulled together as he studied the device in the chief's hand.

Though Amber had worn a black button-down shirt, as the chief had suggested, she still worried the little black microphone would stick out like a neon "We're recording every word you say because we think you murdered your mistress!" sign.

But Amber had a spell for that.

The chief went over the questions—again—that he suggested Amber work into the conversation. Given the public, and now widely talked about, breakup of the Sadlers' marriage, the chief was less sure of how open to talking Derrick would be. The secret word she was supposed to say if things started to get hairy was "quagmire." If she said it, the chief and one of his officers—not Carl—would come in to help her.

It wasn't as if the chief thought Derrick was going to start brandishing deadly weapons if Amber got too personal with her questions, but it calmed her nerves to know the chief was planning for the worst-case scenario, just in case.

"I'll be next door," Chief Brown said, finally relinquishing his hold on the recording device. It reminded Amber of the mics she saw occasionally dislodged from the waistbands of celebrities on talk shows.

Carl wrinkled his nose. "It's too bad there isn't a pub next to the Sadler building, huh, boss? You're stuck doing your sting operation in the Milk Bowl. Ugh. I don't have a problem with healthy stuff or anything but, like, everything in there has wheatgrass in it. Just 'cause we like cats in Edgehill doesn't mean we have to eat like them, am I right, boss?" He gave the chief a playful nudge with his elbow. "A pint of Cat Scratch IPA would be sa-weet though. Too bad you can't have that instead."

Chief Brown just stared at Carl while he rambled on, face expressionless and mouth pressed into a straight line. "Out."

Carl blinked rapidly, then glanced at Amber. "What'd I say?"

In a stage whisper, she said, "I think drinking on the job is against the rules."

"Oooh," Carl said, thunking himself in the forehead with the heel of his palm. "That's right, that's right."

"Paperwork, Carl," the chief said.

"Yeah, okay, sure," Carl said, grinning. "Good luck, Amber! Get something on him so we can nail that bastard to the wall!"

The chief pinched the bridge of his nose.

Carl saluted and left, unfazed.

Amber smothered a smile.

"Please don't encourage him," the chief said.

"Oh, he's harmless. Enthusiastic," said Amber.

"Unprofessional."

"He's young. He'll outgrow it."

The chief harrumphed. Then his gaze shifted to her chest before quickly looking away. "I ... do you need help getting the wire on? There aren't many women working today, but I could ask Dolores."

Dolores had to be Sour Face. Amber imagined her hands were as cold as ice cubes. She was mortified just thinking about it. "No, I'll be okay. We can test it out before I go in, to make sure it works."

He pursed his lips, eyeing her. "Are you sure you're okay with this?"

"Absolutely."

"Your … ability would tell you if something wasn't right here, wouldn't it? You can sense danger?"

What did he think she was, psychic?

She tried not to laugh at herself.

Yesterday, she'd told Chief Brown about seeing maybe-Derrick behind Melanie's house. How he'd shushed her. How she and Nicolette had chased after him. And she'd finally given him the note Nicolette had found on her car. She appreciated his concern, if nothing else. It was better than the alternative.

"Yes, I'll be fine," she said. "If he's responsible for this, I wanna help nail the bastard to the wall."

The chief let out a bark of laughter that surprised them both.

Smiling, Amber walked out of the interrogation room, device clasped firmly in her hand.

Amber had enough time to pop into the Milk Bowl and use their restroom. She needed it partly to splash cold water on her face and to give her wild-eyed reflection a pep talk. But she also needed the privacy of a stall to get the device properly installed on her person. Because the Edgehill station's tech wasn't exactly state-of-the-art, Amber didn't have an earpiece to allow for information to be transmitted to her from the chief while she was talking to Derrick. All she could do was turn the thing on. She did that now, sliding the little tab from off to on, and watched as a small green light illuminated on the black box.

She removed her shirt and wedged the wire under the bottom of her bra. It took some finagling, once her shirt was back on, to get the little microphone to stick out of the space between two of her buttons.

"Hello?" she said softly.

Her phone pinged.

"Hear you loud and clear," the text said.

Amber stepped out of the stall and checked her reflection again. The microphone was half the size of a dime, but the gray head might as well have been a manhole cover on her chest, for how conspicuous it looked.

Flicking her gaze to the bathroom door, Amber thought of her magicked blackboard. It was a spell about rearranging what was already there. A manipulation of concrete materials. Glamour spells—her sister's forte, not hers—didn't manipulate anything but a person's *perception* of a thing.

Amber did a quick spell that manipulated the mesh head of the microphone to resemble a tiny flower. Now it looked like a very small decorative pin.

"Still with me?" she said out loud.

Her phone in her hand pinged almost immediately. "Perfect."

"Okay," she said, running her sweaty palms down the length of her shirt. "Let's do this."

It wasn't one of Amber's better pep talks, but it would have to do.

She strolled confidently out of the Milk Bowl's bathroom. Chief Brown and another officer—one closer to his age—sat at a table near the door. Amber vaguely remembered him being introduced yesterday as "Garcia." The chief's laptop was open. He had his headphones on, back facing her, while Garcia read a book. A plate of what looked like rice cakes was on the table, alongside two small glasses filled with a sludgy dark-green liquid that could only be pulverized wheatgrass shots. Amber's nose wrinkled. Maybe Carl was right.

The chief didn't look behind him as she walked past, but Garcia looked up from his book for long enough to nod at her slightly before resuming his reading. Amber let her gaze skip over them as if they were mere pieces of furniture. A text came through just as she stepped outside.

"Remember," the text said, "if you run into a quagmire, let me know."

Amber nodded to herself and slipped her phone into her purse without replying.

The Sadler Accounting office was the next building over and it took her all of ten seconds to reach the door, the company's name written in a crisp white font on the glass. As she pushed it open, she was greeted with warm air tinged with the scent of cinnamon. A three-wick, rust-colored candle sat on the reception desk, the flames dancing slowly in their glass enclosure. A cheery receptionist—a girl who couldn't have been older than eighteen or nineteen—stood when Amber entered the lobby.

"Hi there," she said. "You must be—" she glanced down at something Amber couldn't see, surrounded as she was by the tall barrier of the desk "—uhh. Oh shoot." The girl winced and bit down on her bottom lip, then looked back up, big brown eyes wide. "Amber Blackwood? Mr. Sadler's noon appointment?"

Amber wondered why the girl looked two seconds from passing out. "Yep, that's me," she said, absently gripping the handle of her leather over-the-shoulder bag. The inside of her forearm bumped against something misshapen in her purse. She'd almost forgotten all about the peacock toy she'd made for Sydney.

"Okay. Uhh …" the girl said, frantically scratching the side of her nose with her pointer finger. A nervous tic, clearly. "Just have a seat and Mr. Sadler will … uh … be out to see you shortly."

The girl's behavior wasn't helping Amber's own nerves. She perched herself awkwardly on the edge of a blue-gray chair, purse placed on top of her knees, which were tightly squeezed together.

When Amber had devised this plan with the chief, it had made perfect sense. Just have a set of questions to work into the conversation. She hadn't accounted for the panic she'd feel when she had a wire strapped to her. The chief would be able to hear *everything* she said. Could he hear how hard her heart was beating? The sound would surely drown out everything else.

What if she was so nervous, that once she was actually talking to Derrick, she started to blurt out nonsense? What if she panic-confessed to being a witch? What if she couldn't say anything at all?

She wasn't sure the chief would react well to her confession, considering how mystified he was by her supposed psychic abilities.

Amber tried to calm herself by taking in her surroundings and breathing deeply. She imagined the chief wincing at every one of her gusty exhales, but her phone didn't light up with text messages begging her to stop.

The lobby had enough room for three gray-blue chairs— one of which she was currently perched on—a potted plant with browning edges, and a water cooler. The clock on the wall next to her slowly tick, tick, ticked away the seconds. Amber wasn't sure what to ask Derrick to make it sound like this was a meeting solely about her business. She had no desire to expand. It was too risky to ship charmed toys all over the country. All she would need was a toy's magic-infused disc to malfunction and cause a problem.

Scarlet the dragon had originally had a tiny disc implanted in her throat that had been overlaid with a fire spell so she could breathe tiny balls of fire—only to be used in elaborate demonstrations at the Here and Meow, of course. Selling fire-breathing dragon toys to children was a recipe for disaster. And arson.

The first time Amber had tested out Scarlet's new ability, the dragon had let out a huge blast of flame that not only melted the dragon immediately, but set the curtains in Amber's apartment on fire. She figured that was the real reason Tom no longer trusted her animated creations.

She felt someone's gaze on her now, and found the receptionist watching her from behind her desk. From Amber's spot in the lobby, all she could see of the receptionist was her forehead and wide eyes.

What on earth was the matter with the girl?

Just then, the door into the lobby from the other side of the reception desk swung open. Derrick strode out with a gym bag slung over his shoulder, a pair of sunglasses hanging from the collar of his shirt, and a ball cap on his head. Absolute certainty hit her like a truck. It had definitely been Derrick outside Melanie's house Sunday morning.

Amber immediately jumped to her feet. Derrick stopped dead in his tracks.

He was even more handsome in person. For a brief moment, she understood what had taken Melanie in. The physique, the confident posture, the chiseled jaw.

They stared at each other.

The receptionist shrank so low into her shoulders, Amber was surprised she hadn't pulled her head completely into her torso, like a turtle.

"Uhh ... hi, Miss Blackwood," Derrick finally said. His gaze darted from his receptionist to Amber and back again.

"I'm sorry, Mr. Sadler," the girl squeaked, then bit down on her thumb. "I ... I must have ..."

Glancing at Amber, he held up a finger, and then said, "One ... one second, okay?" When he turned back to the receptionist, he leaned over the top of the desk, just slightly, and then quietly gave the young girl a dressing down.

Amber couldn't hear most of what was said, but she caught snatches of it. "Cancel" and "forgetful" and "warning" made it to her ears.

Amber's phone buzzed in her purse, but she didn't dare take it out.

Finally, Derrick turned and offered Amber a tight-lipped smile. "Sorry about that, Amber. My assistant forgot to cancel today's meeting. I …" He glanced down at himself, and though it was clear that whatever he said next would almost assuredly be a lie, he soldiered on anyway. "I have an appointment elsewhere."

They both knew his only appointment was with a treadmill.

"It won't take very long." Amber couldn't *not* talk to him now, not when she had an increasingly warm battery-powered listening device strapped to her, a police chief listening in from the place next door, and a very intricately designed toy in her bag. No, he would talk to her. And he would talk to her today. "I'm really anxious to start working with an accountant before the Here and Meow. It would be the best time to advertise my expanding business. I need to set up an online store and I don't know what all this might cost …"

Derrick hadn't spoken, but at least now he didn't look like a sprint for the door was inevitable.

"Besides, if you can't meet with me today, I'll have to go to Welson and Howell."

That was a name the chief had given her when he'd briefed her on what topics to cover during her chat with Derrick.

The man's lip curled. "You'd go to *Marbleglen*?"

"I'm desperate," Amber said, adding a helpless shrug. "But if you're too busy because of your impending—" she gave him an elevator scan "—appointment, I can leave." She made a move like she was heading for the door.

Derrick sighed, then shook his head, wincing slightly. "Come on back." Then he turned to his receptionist. "Cancel everything else on my schedule if you haven't already done so, Ashley. After the weekend I had, I … I just can't, okay?" He shot another tight-lipped smile at Amber. "Right this way, Miss Blackwood."

Derrick opened the door he'd come out of earlier, his gym bag now held at his side rather than flung over his shoulder. Amber followed behind him, her thoughts a jumbled mess. She was glad the chief's listening device wasn't hardwired to her brain. The questions and topics the chief had suggested were flitting around her strategies for getting the peacock toy out of her bag and into Derrick's hands. Once she got him to hold it, could she ask him, pointblank, if he had killed Melanie? Whatever she asked, he would have to answer. Would her magic, and the use of the code word, be enough to save her, should Derrick retaliate?

She and Derrick walked down a narrow hallway, doors on both sides. Amber wondered how many accountants worked at Sadler Accounting. No light shone behind any of the doors. No voices could be heard. Was everyone out to lunch? Amber wondered if any of the employees had left Sadler Accounting once their boss became part of a murder investigation.

When they reached the third door on the right, Derrick

turned the knob on a door labeled with his name, and the words "Head Accountant" written beneath it.

His office was tidy, the space eaten up by a ridiculously large desk. Given the small room and the narrow hallway, she had to assume the thing had been assembled inside. It wouldn't leave again unless it was in pieces. It was made of sleek and shiny cherrywood and was shaped like a giant L. It had a hutch on one side, lined with mesh boxes stacked with papers and folders. A large monitor sat on one side of the desk, with a stack of folders and other various papers on the other.

Derrick motioned for Amber to take a seat in one of the two chairs on the other side of his desk, while he rounded the side of the L's shorter arm. He dropped his gym bag in an unseen corner and then sat in his black leather desk chair. Peeling off his baseball cap, he placed it on the desk, near the monitor. It was too far away to touch, but close enough that she could see every detail of the roaring tiger's face, its extended paw, and the words "Roaring Tiger Little League" scrawled beneath it.

Derrick rolled forward a few inches, redirecting her attention, and placed his folded arms on the desk's surface. He smiled, strained as it was. "So, what are your main concerns?"

"Uhh …"

I'm worried you killed my friend. I'm concerned that your wife is seconds from falling apart.

"About expanding your business, I mean," he said, as if he'd read her mind.

Oh, that. Well, I'm worried one of my spells will misfire and cause a major catastrophe and someone will find out I'm a witch and I'll be burned at the stake—or whatever happens to witches these days ...

"Miss Blackwood?"

"Umm ... mostly I'm worried about shipping costs," she said, plucking an answer out of thin air. "When I keep the business localized to Edgehill, I don't have to transport the product anywhere."

He'd pulled out a notepad while she talked and scribbled down a few lines. "Those are valid concerns. Have you ..."

Amber tuned him out then, as he went over things like "projected sales numbers" and "gains and losses." She mentally sifted through the chief's conversation suggestions. She also needed to find a logical time to pull the peacock out of her bag.

As he continued to talk, and Amber nodded where she thought appropriate, she slowly inched her hand into her bag and closed her fingers around the body of the peacock, its feathers closed now.

"There's definitely a market for your creations though, Amber. You're a very talented toymaker. I would be more than happy to help you figure out the best way to keep your costs low."

"Thank you," she said, realizing this was her in. "You said Sydney really liked the duck toy?"

Derrick leaned back in his chair a bit, smiling. The chance to talk about his love of numbers seemed to have softened him a bit to the idea of chatting with her. "Oh yes. She absolutely loves the duck. We got it for her a couple years ago, so the battery in it has died by now." His head tottered back and forth as he clearly debated how best to say what came next. "Now, I don't want to tell you how to run your business, please keep that in mind, but creating the toys so it's possible to dismantle them enough to swap in a new battery will give your toys more longevity. Sydney has such fond memories of that duck. It often travels with her. But, of course, she's thrilled to get a new one each year. Maybe your methods are actually ingenious and keep kids—and their parents—coming back for more."

Amber managed a tight-lipped smile similar to the one he'd angled at her in the lobby. "I actually brought a new one for Sydney as a thank-you for meeting with me."

"Oh, that wasn't necessary," he said.

Amber placed the bird on his desk and formed the question she needed in her mind.

Derrick's eyes lit up as if he himself were a twelve-year-old and not a grown man. "Wow, Amber. It's truly beautiful."

"If you pick it up and say the command, you can activate its tail."

"You know, I have to say, the way you've incorporated voice activation into your creations is truly impressive." But he only stared at the toy, keeping his hands clasped in his lap. "These toys are fairly sturdy, but something like this one, with so many moving parts, you'll likely need custom packaging for each design. Something with a plastic window to showcase your craftsmanship would make sense. Have you priced out things like this yet? What kind of budget—"

"I don't know, honestly," Amber said. "About any of these things. Melanie was in the process of helping me with it, but …"

Derrick nodded. "I was sorry to hear about her passing."

Amber stifled an eye roll. "Did you know her well? She and Whitney were on the Here and Meow Committee together so I wondered if—"

He sighed, working his jaw. "Is that why you're here? To talk about Melanie? Did my wife send you?"

His tone had lost what little bit of professional cheer he'd mustered up for her.

"No one sent me," she said, which wasn't exactly true. Her gaze skittered over to the roaring tiger on his hat, and the memory of him shushing her came back. *He* was really going to get testy with *her*? "Why were you behind her house Sunday morning?"

His jaw clenched.

"You're just going to pretend that didn't happen? That I didn't see you?"

"This isn't the time or place, Miss Blackwood," he said, hands going to his armrests, like he was gearing to stand up. To dismiss her. To usher her out of his office.

She needed to get him to stay, but all her crafted questions and talking points had flown out of her head. "I planned to go to the police about seeing you there."

That got his attention, hands still on the armrests, looking like a cricket about to launch skyward. "What?"

"It really made me—and Nicolette, Melanie's mother— uncomfortable that you were outside Melanie's house. The police said to come to them with any concerns. I think you creeping around the house of your dead mistress is pretty concerning."

Amber wasn't sure where all that had come from, but she

tried to keep her face blank. She wanted Derrick to know she was serious.

He folded his hands on the desk again. "And, what, you came here to warn me first?"

"I wanted to give you a chance to explain yourself," she said. "You're their prime suspect, aren't you?"

Amber's phone buzzed. Yeah, yeah, she'd gone off the rails. But Derrick was listening to her.

"They've talked to you a bunch of times, I'm guessing," she said. "It's always someone who was close to the victim. I'm guessing an affair would make you pretty close."

His face was starting to turn red, the color slowly licking up his neck and into his face like a slow-moving inferno. "What do you want me to say, Amber? Yes, I was having an affair. Whatever your moral position on that is, and whether or not you believe this, I loved Melanie. I truly did. I was behind her house because I run past there every morning. I miss her, okay?"

"I heard Whitney found out."

He sighed heavily, four of his fingers massaging slow strokes across his temple, his eyes closed for a moment. "Yeah, well, everyone has heard that by now."

When he looked at her again, dropping his hand, his eyes were … sad. The angry tint of his face had started to recede. His gaze fell on the peacock still waiting patiently on his desk. Tentatively, he picked up the toy and placed its feet on his open palm. In a distant, soft voice, he asked, "What was the command?"

"Indigo, walk."

Derrick repeated the command and the peacock came to life, shaking his head as if waking from a dream. Indigo shook his tail feathers too, causing the plastic bunch to sweep slowly back and forth across Derrick's skin.

He managed a smile. "Truly remarkable. Sydney will love it."

As he was carefully placing the bird onto his desk, Amber knew she had to ask her question, and soon. The truth spell would run out after a minute. If she didn't ask something now, she would lose her chance. "Did you kill Melanie?"

Without pause, he said, "No."

Amber's eyes widened. If it hadn't been him, who was responsible?

Derrick was too focused on Indigo to see the distressed look on her face. A look that should have comforted a grieving friend. He watched as the plastic bird started its sauntering walk across folders and papers.

"Where … where were you the morning she died?"

He squinted at her, crossing his arms. "I discussed all this with the police already. Why not just ask them? You're planning to report me anyway, aren't you? It doesn't matter how many times I tell them I didn't kill her, they seem to have their minds made up." He paused, glaring at her. "Sounds like you have, too."

There was a hollow feeling in Amber's chest. She'd walked in here so sure she was talking to Melanie's killer. But a truth spell couldn't be outsmarted. It wasn't like a polygraph. Truth spells uncovered the truth, plain and simple.

Derrick hadn't killed Melanie.

Which meant that the killer was still roaming the streets of Edgehill.

"I loved her too," Amber said, her voice catching on the last word.

Derrick sagged a little in his seat. It took him a while to finally say, "Whitney and I had gotten into a fight the day before—about finances, funnily enough—and I'd left to stay at a friend's house in Belhaven. I wasn't even in Edgehill when it happened."

That sounded like a rather airtight alibi to Amber. Why did the chief still think Derrick was their guy?

"Problem is," Derrick said, "my buddy has been out of town for weeks on a business trip overseas. I have a key to his place, so I just crashed there. No one was there to confirm it. And Whitney was with Sydney early that morning, shuttling her around to whatever her new hobby is. Fashion now, I think? So she wasn't home to corroborate my story or confirm when I came home. By the time Whitney dropped Sydney off at school and got back to Edgehill, Melanie was … she was already …" He shook his head. "What a mess."

Amber's stomach was still in knots. "I just have one more question."

Derrick laughed a humorless laugh. "What?"

"Did Melanie ask you to leave Whitney?"

"Once," he said.

"When you worked at Northwind Consultants together?"

He stared at her for a long moment. "Yes. But that was over a decade ago."

"Do you think she relocated to Edgehill for you?"

"What, are you a private detective now?"

"A concerned friend."

Derrick ran a quick hand through his hair. "We'd kept in touch over the years. Nothing significant; we didn't see each other. We sent a lot of messages and texts though. We used that app where the messages disappear after a couple minutes?"

"Snapchat?" Amber asked.

"Yeah, that," he said. "Anyway, I was just as shocked as anyone else when Mel showed up in Edgehill one day. She didn't throw herself at me or anything. But … I don't know … we just fell back into things. She didn't ask me to leave Whitney this time. We just … saw each other when we could."

"And Whitney never suspected anything?"

"Not that I know of. And Whitney's the type to let you know," he said. "What Mel and I had was great for what it was, but neither one of us was ready for what it meant if we decided to make a go at a legitimate relationship. But …"

"But what?" she asked, when he didn't say anything else for several long seconds.

"A couple days before she died … she called me for the first time in a while. We usually stuck to texts. She sounded … off? I can't explain it. Something was bothering her and she asked to see me. I was busy and distracted when she called, so I didn't get back to her right away." He frowned. "The night she died was the same day I'd had that fight with Whitney. That afternoon, I texted Melanie that I'd be in Belhaven for the night and she could talk to me there. Said we'd have the whole house to ourselves."

"Did she meet you?"

192

He shook his head. "I never heard from her again. Calls and texts went unanswered, which wasn't like her. I figured she'd gotten sick again. I should have gone to see her, but I was worried someone would see me and it would get back to Whitney." Frowning, he said, "Not knowing what she wanted to talk to me about has been eating me up. What could she have needed to tell me that she couldn't say over the phone?"

Amber wished she knew.

"And for the record, if Melanie *had* asked me to leave Whitney … I mean, if she'd asked me again," he said, "I would have done it in a heartbeat."

CHAPTER 14

When Derrick's assistant knocked on the door and poked her head inside, Amber took that as her cue to leave. Her heart ached, her stomach was upset, and she needed fresh air.

"I'll walk you out," Derrick said, standing. He put his hands in the pockets of his workout pants, then pulled them out. Crossed his arms.

"That's okay," Amber said, hiking her purse onto her shoulder. "I can see myself out. I hope Sydney likes Indigo!"

And then she was slipping past the young receptionist and down the narrow hallway and out the door to the lobby. She cast a quick glance into the windows of the Milk Bowl as she went by, but kept moving. Her cell rang.

"Hi, chief," she said in greeting, still walking down the sidewalk.

"Hi, Amber," he said. "Were Melanie and Susie Paulson close friends?"

Amber's forehead scrunched up. Susie's name hadn't even come up during that conversation. "What? What does that—"

"Humor me," he said. "Something Derrick said got us thinking."

"Uh … not that I know of," Amber said. "We all knew each

other well enough because of Here and Meow, but Melanie and Susie weren't chummy. Why?"

"Around the same time we sent in the vial found in Melanie's hand, I sent a few items from Paws 4 Tea to the lab in Portland."

Amber stopped walking in the middle of the sidewalk and someone clipped her arm. They both apologized and Amber pressed herself against the wall of the nearest building to get out of the way of foot traffic. The street was full of people heading back to their offices after lunch. She spotted the chief walking out of the Milk Bowl and across the street. He didn't look her way. Garcia walked out a few seconds later, also on the phone.

What the chief had just said finally caught up to her brain.

She knew now, that aside from herself and Derrick, Susie Paulson had been on the police's very short list of suspects since the beginning. But why? Being grumpy wasn't enough to plop someone into the middle of a murder investigation.

Why do you think Susie, of all people, had something to do with it? was what she wanted to say, but would Psychic Amber say that? *Think. They specifically sent in tea. The tea is what's significant here.*

Then Amber remembered one of the last things Melanie had said to her. "*No more tea, though. I'm so sick of it. If one more person brings me tea, so help me …*"

Was Susie one of those people who had brought Melanie tea? Amber flashed back to the Here and Meow meeting where Susie had accused Amber of poisoning patrons. Had Susie's guilty conscience crept in and forced her to indirectly confess?

"It wouldn't be outside Susie's capabilities to harm Melanie if it suited her ambitions," Psychic Amber said. "She's been desperate to land the position of head director of the Here and Meow for years. She's been acting odd lately; her alliances have shifted. She's suddenly become more friendly with people she actively avoided only months ago."

Amber hoped she'd said enough to convince him to keep talking.

The chief hmmed his agreement. "We'd already received an early tip—a couple, actually—from a few of Susie's coworkers at the tea shop. One girl said Susie had been creating a care package for Melanie in the storeroom, since she'd been so sick on and off for weeks. The girl came in needing chamomile tea and grabbed one of the last few boxes that had been sitting near the basket Susie was putting together. Susie lunged at her and snatched the box back and said it was for Melanie and Melanie only."

Amber leaned heavily against the wall, her head tipped back so her skull touched the cool brick behind her. "Being overly concerned about people really isn't Susie's way. It's strange she went to the trouble."

"Exactly," the chief said. "We found discarded teabags in Melanie's trash and in the sink that we collected and sent to the lab for any traces of poisonous substances. Sounds like I need to call in a rush order on that." She watched as he climbed into his car. "I've got to go."

She noted that he'd clearly put in a rush order on the vial from her store, as those results had already come in. He'd been more suspicious of her than he'd been of Susie. She tried not to let that sting.

"Are you … are you going to go arrest Susie?"

"Can't. All we have is circumstantial evidence at this point. We need the results from the lab."

Amber wondered if the toxicology report from Melanie's autopsy had come in. Maybe that needed to be rushed, too. "Oh, I still have the … device," she said, looking down at the flower-shaped microphone head poking out from between her buttons. She'd have to change that back.

"Drop it back off at the station. Dolores is expecting you."

The call ended and the chief's car pulled out of its space. Garcia followed close behind.

Amber needed a secure place to de-wire herself. Diagonally across from her stood Clawsome Coffee. It wasn't her first choice for coffee, but she desperately needed something hot snaking through her system. She only hoped the steadily coursing adrenaline wouldn't react badly to the caffeine. She crossed the street and slipped inside the noisy shop. Amber also hoped old Paulette Newsom wasn't working today.

She was, as Larry Terrence had said, a she-demon.

Clawsome didn't have the sleek, modern feel of Purrcolate, but there was something inherently Edgehill about the place. Warm and inviting. The walls and furniture were all made of polished, well-worn wood. It smelled like coffee, of course, but also like vanilla and cinnamon and something sharp and rich Amber could never quite put her finger on, try as she might to name the elusive scent.

She quickly ducked into the restroom and divested herself

of the device, magicked the microphone back to normal, then shoved it all into her purse.

Once back in the main part of the shop, Amber inhaled deeply, walking toward the counter, then almost choked when she saw Clawsome's owner, Paulette, manning the register. Despite being in her late sixties, and having a daughter willing and able to take over the business—or at least to take some of the everyday responsibilities off Paulette's shoulders—Paulette had started working even more hours once Purrcolate opened up across town. Amber had a suspicion that Paulette thought if her customers saw her face every day, it would help remind them to stay loyal and not sell out to the glitz and glamor of a place with Wi-Fi.

"Oh, Amber, *dear*, how are you?" Paulette asked when it was Amber's turn to place her order. Only Paulette could make the word "dear" sound like an insult.

"I'm doing okay, Paulette," she said, trying not to let any hint of rudeness seep into her tone. "How are you?"

"Can't complain, can't complain," she said, though her tight-lipped smile hinted that complaining was the only thing that truly brought her joy in this life and it was specifically Amber's fault that she couldn't. "What'll it be today?"

Amber always ordered the same thing. "A large mocha, please."

"Coming right up, love!"

Amber idled near the cart piled high with sugars, creams, stirring straws, and napkins. The café was only half full at this hour, mostly older men playing cards or young girls sitting in pairs, chatting quietly.

When her order was ready, Paulette called out Amber's name, but didn't immediately hand over the cup. "Can I ask you something, love?"

Give me strength …

Amber just wanted her coffee and to get back to the Quirky Whisker. An order for a dozen cat toys for a girl's sleepover birthday party had been placed yesterday and Amber hadn't even started on them yet. It would be the perfect task to get lost in instead of dwelling on the fact that Susie Paulson had possibly poisoned Melanie. "Of course."

"Well," she said, looking from side to side to make sure no one was listening, and then leaned forward, keeping her voice low. Amber bent forward to catch what she said next. "I heard something about your friend Melanie."

Amber's jaw clenched. She should just walk away. Paulette was baiting her and she knew it. Melanie had chosen Purrcolate to provide pastries to the participants of the Here and Meow 5k and Paulette had never forgiven her.

"Complete the race and get a complimentary scone from Purrcolate!" the stack of flyers in Melanie's office had said.

Clawsome Coffee had been the provider of after-race treats for years, and then Melanie had swept in and taken the gig from Paulette. Paulette's ability to hold a grudge was awe-inspiring. Clearly, it didn't matter if the object of her scorn was no longer of this earth.

Rumor had it that Paulette had a sister she'd lost touch with because Paulette was sure her sister had stolen her favorite dress in high school—and then had caught the eye of the most popular guy at Edgehill High, whom she'd later married.

Paulette was convinced all of that would have happened to her, had *she* been wearing the dress that day.

Amber found that hard to believe, considering Paulette had the personality of an old moose.

"I hear she'd been siphoning money from the Here and Meow treasury," Paulette said now, clearly pleased with herself. "She had a bit of a racy history, did you know?" She sniffed once and gave Amber's entire person a quick scan from head to toe without lifting her head. "*You* were friends with her. I'm sure you knew. But I heard she'd been having an affair with a married man in whatever fancy city she'd been living in and the wife found out and ran her out. So she came here and brought her sinful behavior with her. Can you imagine stealing from the Here and Meow? It was probably to pay off those Terrence brothers. I always donated my pastries for free, you know, but I heard they insisted on being paid. Can you—"

"You know what, Paulette? Keep the coffee." Amber tossed her purse over her shoulder and stomped out of the café, feeling her magic pulsing and writhing beneath her skin.

Really? *Really?* A woman was dead and Paulette was still upset about her *pastries*?

Amber considered it a small miracle that she'd made it out of there before she upended the drink on Paulette's head.

As Amber did her best to calm her racing heart and her racing magic, eyes focused on her black flats, she slammed into someone. Again. It knocked her emotionally heightened magic down a peg, at least.

A pair of hands held her arms to steady her. "Whoa, you okay?"

Her head snapped up at the sound of his voice. It was Connor Declan.

Amber flushed, body tensing. "Geez, I'm sorry! I wasn't paying attention to where I was going."

Connor let go.

It was then that she noticed a battered paperback on the ground by their feet. Amber reached down to pick it up before Connor could.

It was a fantasy novel, from what she could tell. And given the title and the silhouette of the buxom woman in a tall pointy hat leaning against a tree, Amber guessed the main character was a witch.

Connor quickly took the book from her hands without actually snatching it away. He held it to his chest, cover pressed to his shirt. "I guess I wasn't looking where I was going either."

"Were you walking and reading?"

He laughed. "Bad habit."

They fell silent for a moment.

Her magic thrummed. Her anger, too. Rising up in her like a tide. Anger at Paulette. At Derrick and Susie and even Melanie, a little. Though she wasn't sure why. Maybe because she missed her and was angry she was gone.

Connor was a sudden, unexpected distraction. An even better one than the dozen cat toys she needed to make.

"So," she said, "is that a really old copy from the library or ..."

"Uh ..." He flushed, pulling the cover away from him long enough to stare at it before pressing it to him again and looking up at her. "It's my favorite book. I reread it every winter. It's ... my thirteenth year in a row reading it."

"Wow," she said, impressed. "What do you like about it so much that you'll read it that many times when you already know what will happen?"

Smiling, he relaxed a little. "Oh, Amber, don't you know? It's the journey that matters, not the destination."

"Yet, it's the same journey you've already taken a dozen times," she said. "Do you experience something new every time?"

"Yeah," he said. "Every read is different. I'll find a line that resonates with me in a way that it never has before. Or events that I can relate to, now that I'm older. Parts that make me cringe a little because it's outdated, but still make me happy because of the fond memories."

Amber was jealous. She'd never read a book she loved so dearly that she wanted to reread it over and over.

Connor cleared his throat, dropping his hands to his side, one still holding close to the book. "Where were you headed in such a hurry?"

Lip curled, Amber glanced over her shoulder at Clawsome Coffee. Paulette stood at a floor-to-ceiling window, watching her, arms crossed. She glared at Amber. As if *Amber* was the one at fault here. The nerve. Amber turned back to face Connor, her blood—and her magic—starting to boil again. "More like I was trying to get *away* quickly."

Connor glanced around her and presumably spotted grumpy old Paulette because he raised a hand in greeting. Then he winced and dropped it. "She just used a rather obscene hand gesture. How terribly rude."

Amber laughed at his overly affected tone, unable to help herself. "Where were *you* headed?"

"I was walking over to Angora Threads. I'm doing a piece on them for the *Gazette*."

"I've always wanted to see that place," she said, surprised by her own admission. When her cheeks heated, she considered sprinting in the other direction.

"Did you … uh … want to come with me?" he asked.

"I … umm … yes? Yes. Sure. Thanks."

"Oh!" he said, seemingly as surprised by this turn of events as she was. "Well, right this way …" With an overdone flourish of his hand, she turned and headed back the short way she'd come after she'd barreled out of Clawsome Coffee. Connor fell into step beside her.

Thankfully, Paulette had gone back into the shop and was no longer glaring at passersby.

The walk to Angora Threads would take them at least fifteen minutes, and the first half of it passed in semi-awkward silence. Connor had been so chatty when he'd come by her shop the other day; why was he clamming up now? Did he have to have a story between him and the other party in the conversation in order to feel comfortable? Or had his confession about his well-loved book thrown him off his game?

Amber supposed he could sense the odd energy coming off her too, and thought it wise to just stay quiet while Amber brooded. The anger slowly started to creep back in. She beat it back.

"So what's your story about?" she asked.

He jumped slightly, as if he'd been so lost in his own

thoughts, he'd forgotten she was there. "Well, this year they're also having a junior fashion show."

"I heard about that," Amber said. "I don't know much about it."

"They accepted kids between twelve and eighteen. Winner gets the same prize as the adult winners: a yearlong apprenticeship at Angora Threads and a thousand-dollar prize. Depending on the age of the winner, the internship might have to be done remotely, of course."

"Wow. What made them decide to have a junior fashion show this year too?" she asked.

"Apparently, Letty—you know, the owner?—her son, Diego, is a whiz at creating clothes. One day she came home to find he'd made a vintage dress—you know with that kind of apron-like neck part?"

Amber laughed. "A halter?"

"Yeah, that," he said, looking at her for a moment, before quickly looking away and focusing his attention back on his feet as he walked. "Anyway, Diego made this perfectly crafted vintage halter dress using some of the abundantly available cat-print fabric. Letty loved it and posted it on Angora Threads' social media, more as a 'Look at how talented my kid is!' than anything else. Next thing she knew, requests for the dress started pouring in. The demand for it was so high, she put several of her seamstresses to the task of making *only* that dress for several months. She had to hire several more people to her staff. And she more or less hired her sixteen-year-old kid to work for her, too.

"Others chimed in on her social media and told her that

their kids were talented too and shared pictures of their creations. Letty realized it wasn't fair to keep kids locked out of the internship simply due to age."

"Are they all kids from Edgehill?"

Connor shook his head. "That's the pretty cool thing too. She opened the internship up to the whole nation and has kids from all over participating for four months. It started a couple weeks ago. Sounds like a few of the parents are holed up in the Manx Hotel for three months so their kids can take part. Letty offered a few scholarships so lower-income families could participate too. There are three Edgehill kids in the running, though. One of them is only twelve. I hear she's a prodigy."

Amber thought about all that for a while. "Did you choose this story or was it assigned to you? I can't believe I haven't heard much about it."

Amber spotted the warehouse-like building up ahead.

"When my editor asked us in a staff meeting who was interested, my hand was in the air before she finished the question," Connor said. "I knew I wanted to be a writer from a young age and was lucky enough to have a father who helped me hone my craft. I love the idea of other young kids getting a chance to be trained at something they love."

Amber stared at his profile, at the flood of pink coloring the tips of his ears. He might have lost some—most?—of his hipster, artsy edge from high school, but there was still something disarmingly attractive about him.

He caught her looking and she glanced away. "I think Letty wanted to keep it a secret for as long as possible—but she knows just as well as anyone that secrets don't stay secrets here for long."

True enough.

"Do you think Letty will mind that I'm tagging along?" she asked as they passed into the large shadow cast by the building.

"Nah," he said. "Letty's cool."

Once they reached the black metal security door set into the face of the wholly unremarkable building, Connor pressed the tiny doorbell and took a couple steps back.

In less than a minute, pounding footsteps were followed by a wooden door opening, and then the security door swung toward them. A petite Hispanic woman grinned out at them, her hand still on the doorknob.

"Connor, you made it! Come on in." Then Letty spotted Amber. Thankfully, her smile didn't falter. "Ah, the famous Amber Blackwood! The more the merrier."

Amber thanked her as she followed Connor inside the tiny landing. He immediately started climbing the steps, so Amber followed. Plain gray walls stretched up on either side of them. Amber flinched when Letty closed the security door with a rattling clang, followed by the main one. Then her tiny feet pounded up the steps behind them.

When Amber emerged on the second floor, her mouth dropped open. The top floor of Angora Threads was huge, with tall ceilings and a ton of natural light pouring into the space from the windows lining three of the four walls. The stairs led them to the far right of the space, the left side stretching out across the entire area with no breaks for rooms or walls.

Directly across from them stood tall shelves stuffed with

bolts of fabric, their ends protruding out of their cubbies. They seemed to be arranged not by color, but by animal. There were zebra stripes and cheetah spots and leopard print, but also fabric covered in leaping cats, cat faces, and kittens chasing balls of twine.

"Right this way," Letty said, and headed to the left.

The space was dotted with work stations. Some were just long tables piled with scraps of fabric, scissors, pins, and a sewing machine. Other work stations were pressed up against the wall, the area above it covered in sketches for designs, as well as pictures cut out of magazines to aid in inspiration.

One work station might be in total chaos, while the one next to it was so organized that the spools of thread lining the shelf above it were in rainbow order, scissors hung from little hooks hammered into the wall, and bolts of fabric were stored neatly beneath.

There were a few adults hard at work near the wall of fabric. They looked up when Amber and Connor stepped onto the second floor, waved politely, and then got back to work. Most of the activity in the room came from the other end of the warehouse where the hum and *chink, chink, chink* of sewing machines grew ever louder.

A wall of mostly naked mannequins blocked Amber's view of what they were headed toward.

When Letty, Amber, and Connor rounded the mannequin barrier, Amber saw at least a dozen kids bent over sewing machines, cutting fabric, threading needles, or sketching designs. They each had their own small work table, spaced out four across and three deep. They were all so focused, not one of them looked up from their work until Letty spoke.

"All right, everyone," she said, drawing attention to her almost instantly, despite not raising her voice. When she had all dozen pairs of eyes on her—though the occasional quick glance shifted toward Amber and Connor—Letty said, "This is the reporter I was telling you about, remember? He just wants to see what kind of work you're doing, maybe take a couple pictures of your projects, and ask you a few questions."

"Who's she?" one of the younger boys asked—a pudgy kid, with a full head of red curly hair, who couldn't have been older than fourteen.

"She's my assistant," Connor said immediately.

Amber looked at him askance, but sobered quickly.

A girl gasped. "Aren't you … aren't you the lady who makes the toys?" She was tiny, blonde, and staring at Amber with wide blue eyes.

Recognition kicked her in the gut. It was Sydney Sadler.

"That's me," Amber said, trying her best to school her features.

Sydney's face flushed and she bit her lip. She clearly tried to focus on what Letty was telling the group, but her gaze kept nervously shooting toward Amber.

Connor leaned over and whispered, "It looks like someone has a fan."

After Letty went through a short lesson about—something … Amber honestly wasn't paying attention—the kids got back to work. Letty and Connor conferred for a moment, and she reminded him that all pictures would need to be approved

208

by both Letty and the child's parents before anything went to print.

"Make creative choices," Letty said, waved, then walked back across the studio to join the women on the other side of the room, fast at work.

"Need help with anything?" Amber asked, eyeing Connor.

The kids were all working again, either together in small groups, or on their own. Well, all were working accept Sydney. She was positioned in the second row of tables, at the end.

"Maybe you should go autograph something for her," Connor said, laughing. "She looks like she's going to pass out."

While Connor approached a boy who was painstakingly adding sequins to the front of a shirt in the shape of a cat head, Amber walked over to Sydney. She tried not to laugh when she saw Sydney whisper, "Oh my god, oh my god, oh my god" to herself as she anxiously shook out her hands.

"Hi," Amber said when she reached her.

Sydney let out a little squawk and then covered her mouth. "Oh, I mean, hi." Before Amber could say anything else, Sydney said in a rush, "I love your toys. They're so detailed and beautiful and, like, I know this sounds weird, but they're what made me get into clothes. Fashion, I mean. I like creating stuff and your toys are so artistic, you know? Like not just a plastic replica of an animal—I can tell how much you put into them and I try to keep that in mind when I make my designs." She took a breath.

"Thank you," Amber said, truly touched. "That's very sweet of you to say."

It was then that Amber noticed the infamous duck sitting in the corner of Sydney's workspace. Amber picked it up.

"That was my first one," Sydney said. "I started bringing it with me to my lessons."

Placing the duck back down, Amber said, "If I'd known I'd see you, I wouldn't have given your father your present. I would have given it to you directly."

Sydney blinked once. Twice. "A present? For me?"

"Mmhmm," she said. "I heard you were a fan of the toys, so I made one especially for you."

Sydney went beet red. "Oh my gosh, thank you!"

"I was happy to do it. So what are you working on?"

Some of Sydney's nerves started to melt away as she talked to Amber about her designs. She was focused on a series of skirts at the moment, and struggled to choose which one she should tackle first.

"Personally, I like this one," Amber said, pointing to a drawing of an A-line skirt—with pockets—that had a design on the front reminiscent of a poodle, but with a cat wearing a harness and leash.

Sydney grinned. "That's my favorite one too."

When she suddenly fell silent, Amber looked over at her. The young girl's head was bowed. "What's wrong?"

"That lady ... the one who died?" Sydney asked, quickly glancing away. "She was your friend, huh?"

Amber sighed softly. "Yes."

"My mom and dad fought about her a lot. I don't really know why, but they talked about her a lot even before she died," Sydney said, pushing a lone sequin around the tabletop with her pointer finger. "I'm only home on holidays and for stuff like this and it seems like one of them was always talking about her."

"Did you ever meet her?" Amber asked.

"Once or twice, I think," Sydney said, still pushing the sequin around. "Is she why you went to see my dad?"

When Amber saw how tightly the girl's brows were pulled together, she wondered if she had a better sense of the complicated nature of her parents' marriage than she even knew. Instinct told Sydney to be worried, even if she didn't completely understand why. Had news of the divorce reached her yet?

"Partly," Amber said. "I'm just trying to figure out what happened to her."

Sydney nodded. "My mom said she'd never seen so many police in one place. She went for a walk and was going by that lady's house just when all the cops got there. Said she actually saw the body being taken out ... in a *bag*."

Nausea clawed at Amber's stomach as she forced herself not to picture Melanie in a body bag. Seeing her in the morgue, stiff and blue and cold, had been bad enough.

Then something occurred to her. Something Derrick had said.

"Wait," said Amber. "Wasn't your mom taking you back to school that morning?"

"She was supposed to, but she said she wasn't feeling good, so she had that mean lady drive me."

Amber froze. "What?"

Sydney flinched at Amber's tone and stopped idly pushing the sequin around like it was a miniature toy car. She slowly turned to Amber, slightly hunched into her shoulders as if she worried Amber would strike her. "Did I say something bad?"

"*What* mean lady?"

Sydney swallowed. "She's kind of short. Umm … oh! She works at that tea place that smells like wet socks."

"Susie," Amber said, more to herself.

Why the hell had Susie driven *Whitney's* daughter back to school?

"Sorry, I have to go," Amber said, quickly pushing away from the table and striding toward Connor. Then she quickly doubled back and stood before Sydney's station. The girl watched her with wide eyes. "You're talented. Keep working at it and you'll go far." She tapped the cat skirt. "This one, okay? It'll be great."

Amber told Connor a quick goodbye, thanked him for letting her tag along, and hurried for the exit.

She had a question or two for Susie Paulson.

CHAPTER 15

It took Amber fifteen minutes to get from Angora Threads to where her car was parked near the Milk Bowl, then another fifteen to get to Paws 4 Tea. In that time, she'd started to second guess her decision to confront Susie. Maybe Susie actually was a saint under her prickly exterior. Maybe she was the type of person to bring tea and soup to ill friends, and to drive a friend's daughter to school. A school over an hour away.

Amber pushed open the door to the tea shop and was assaulted by the smell Sydney had accurately described as wet socks, though it was faint. It smelled earthy and familiar to Amber. She'd spent so many hours here during high school.

The walls of Paws 4 Tea were made of red brick and lined with thick wooden shelves. They brimmed with row after row of neatly marked jars. Paws 4 Tea boasted fifty types of tea, custom-made mugs, and a small seating area that allowed for up to a dozen guests.

The cashier counter was a tiny rectangle in the middle of the room, keeping one surrounded by tea and customers at all times. It had been a nightmare when she worked here; no chance to slack off, even for a minute.

The counter was currently unmanned, the store devoid of

clientele. But within seconds, a door to the right, flanked on either side by prepackaged tea, opened and out walked Susie.

She'd had a fake smile on her face when she emerged, gearing up to greet a customer. It immediately slid off her face, like butter down the side of a warm ear of corn. "And to what do I owe this pleasure, Amber?" she asked, voice flat as she made her way to the island counter in the middle of the hardwood floor.

"Would you believe I'm here for tea?"

Susie crossed her arms. "Nope."

Amber walked to the wall on her left, running her fingers over the large, black-sticker labels with tea names scrawled in an elegant white cursive. She stopped at the one marked chamomile. With her back turned to Susie, she said, "Did you hear about Derrick and Whitney?"

"Everyone's heard about Derrick and Whitney."

Amber glanced over her shoulder. "How's Whitney taking it?"

Susie's eyes narrowed slightly. "How should I know?"

Hm. So she's going to lie to me, is she?

On the drive here, Amber had chosen a spell to use. It was similar to the one she'd used on Ericka, the morgue receptionist. But this time, instead of teasing out a guilty pleasure, Amber would ask her magic to unearth a recent regret. She'd consulted her grimoire in the small parking lot outside Paws 4 Tea and worked on getting her intention just right.

Her magic had been thrumming beneath her skin since she walked in, ready to be given a task.

The problem with the recent regret spell, of course, was

that there was no way to gauge what someone's regrets might be. It could be anything from their choice for lunch to their choice of spouse.

Amber turned back to the wall of tea and made slow progress across the floor. She released her magic, telling it to search Susie's mind for her most recent regret—which very well could be starting a conversation with Amber herself. She imagined her magic sliding across the floor toward Susie, curling around her legs, and nuzzling her ankles like a cat.

She continued walking and dragging fingers across labels, all the while instructing her magic to pull that regret from Susie's mind to the tip of her tongue. To prime the information so all that was needed to extract it was a well-worded question.

"Oh, it's just that you and Whitney are friends, aren't you?" Amber asked.

Susie let out a grunt and Amber turned to her. Susie's mouth was bunched up, like she felt ill. "I wouldn't say … friends."

"I would think only a friend would be given permission to drive her daughter to her boarding school an hour away," said Amber.

Susie appeared temporarily stunned, mouth slightly agape. "How do you know about that?"

What do you regret, Susie? Her magic delved a little deeper, sinking farther under the surface.

"I saw Sydney earlier," Amber said. "She said her mom didn't take her back to school that day. You did. I figure if she trusted you with her daughter, she'd confide in you about Derrick. It's what a friend would do."

She nudged her magic again. *Find it.*

215

Susie huffed out a loud, sharp breath. "I regret letting Whitney talk me into any of this."

I knew it! "Into what?"

"I … I didn't mean to say that."

"Some part of you must want to talk about it," Amber said, walking to the island counter, standing in front of Susie now. "You're the one who brought it up."

Susie clenched her jaw, gaze darting all over Amber's face, searching for something. What, Amber didn't know.

Push a little more, she told her magic.

She imagined her blue-smoke magic forming a five-fingered hand. Pictured it touching Susie's shoulder and giving it a gentle shove, like nudging a friend at a party in the direction of a guy she really liked. *Go on. Do it. You'll be fine. You'll regret it if you don't.*

"I never meant for it to go this far." Susie's eyes widened.

"What happened?"

"I just wanted to make her sick. Sick enough that she would have to give up her position on the Here and Meow," Susie said.

Amber clenched her teeth together so hard, they hurt. But she didn't have time to be angry. She needed to keep Susie talking before her magic weakened and retreated. "What did you give her to make her sick?"

Susie whimpered and tipped her head back, heels of her palms pressed to her eyes. "I can't believe I … oh god."

"*Susie.*"

Removing her hands from her eyes, she said, "Eth-ylene glycol."

"What the hell is that?"

"The active ingredient in antifreeze," Susie said. "It's color-less and odorless. I was adding small amounts to the packages of tea I brought her."

. Amber took a step back involuntarily. "You *poisoned* her just so you could head the festival? What made you think it would work? You still had to be voted in."

"Whitney said she'd put in a good word for me," she said. "I've put so much flippin' work into that festival. It's time I got paid respect for it."

. "Do you know how pathetic that sounds?" Amber snapped. "Melanie is *dead* now because you're upset you lost a popularity contest. This isn't high school anymore."

Tears—actual tears—pooled in Susie's eyes. She dropped her chin to her chest. "I know."

"I still don't understand why you drove Sydney ..."

"Whitney found Melanie that morning and called me in a panic," Susie said. "I'd stayed with Melanie that night and ... and I made sure she had more tea. She was up sick most of the night ..."

Amber wanted to strangle her.

"I called Whitney to tell her I thought we needed to stop. That we'd given her too much. She agreed and told me to go to work and that she'd check on Melanie later." Susie swallowed. "While I was at home getting ready, Whitney called me in hysterics saying ... saying she must have overdosed because she was ... because she was dead."

Amber crossed her arms tight across her chest. Told herself not to cry. Not to lash out. "Why didn't you tell any of this to the police?"

"And say what? I've been slowly poisoning someone for weeks and things got out of hand and I accidentally killed her?" she snapped. "I don't exactly want to go to jail, Amber."

Amber rubbed her temples, trying to catalogue everything while combatting how *angry* she was.

"I was ... I was screaming and crying and ... Whitney told me I needed to calm down. She sounded *so* calm. She said I should take Sydney to school," Susie said. "Said getting out of town would help clear my head and keep me from doing anything stupid. She ... she said we got into this together and we'd get out of it together. But she would take me down if I turned on her."

"Why did she have anything to do with this? She wanted to help you get this coveted position this badly?"

Susie sniffed, shrugging. "She was pissed Melanie moved to Edgehill. Said it felt like a slap in the face for her to come here when she'd almost destroyed her marriage twelve years ago. So it was to help me, but also to get revenge."

"And it went too far ..."

Susie's eyes welled with tears again. "Are ... are you going to turn me in?" Her bottom lip shook. "I didn't mean to kill her, Amber. I swear."

Amber pulled her magic back then, and she watched Susie slump a little, as if she felt the magic retreat. Or maybe her confession weighed her down.

Amber didn't know what to do with this. If only the recording device had been on, the chief listening on the other end. The box had been switched off, though, and lay dormant in her purse.

Susie stiffened, her gaze focused on something past Amber's shoulder. Amber turned just as the door behind her opened and in walked Chief Brown. She and the chief gaped at each other a moment as Garcia filed in after him. The chief's gaze shifted back to Susie, dismissing Amber.

"Susie Paulson," the chief said, "I need you to come down to the station for questioning."

"Am … am I under arrest?" Susie asked.

"Not yet, Miss Paulson."

Susie looked to Amber, then the chief, and burst into tears. She let Garcia escort her out of the store, her head bowed. She didn't look at Amber.

When the door closed, Amber and the chief were alone.

"I can't imagine what you're doing here, Miss Blackwood. Didn't we have a discussion about not harassing key suspects without permission?"

"I had … an inkling. It led me here."

He pursed his lips at that.

"The results couldn't have come in from Portland already."

"No," he said. "Whitney Sadler called and confessed everything."

"What do you mean everything?"

"She said Susie killed Melanie, and told Whitney about it in confidence. Whitney said she couldn't hold onto the secret any longer."

Amber was shaking her head before he'd even finished speaking. "It wasn't Susie. I mean, yes, she helped poison Melanie, but she didn't kill her."

The chief crossed his arms. "And why do you say that?"

Amber's hand went to the right side of her neck, just below her ear. "Susie never said anything about the puncture wound. She thinks the laced tea alone is what killed her."

"So who killed Melanie, then?"

"The same woman who just called in her confession and threw her supposed friend under the bus."

CHAPTER 16

"Explain," the chief said. "Why do you like Whitney for this now? A couple hours ago, you were convinced it was her husband."

Before the chief could question the validity of Amber's psychic abilities, she told him everything she'd just learned from Susie. "Whitney's alibi this whole time—and something Derrick corroborated because he didn't know any better—was that she'd been taking Sydney back to school over an hour away at the time of Melanie's death. But it was *Susie* who drove Sydney to school. I'm sure there's a way to confirm that; there have to be other witnesses."

The chief just stared at her for a moment. "Come with me."

He turned on his heel and strode out of the tea shop. She hesitated only a moment before she hurried after him. Motioning to his awaiting cop car—the one with Susie in it had already left—Amber got inside. She was in the passenger seat this time, rather than being sequestered to the back seat like a criminal.

They were a full ten minutes into the car ride when Amber said, "Where are we going?"

"To the station," he said. "I'm going to question Susie and

you're going to observe behind the two-way mirror. You can use your … skills to assess whether she's lying."

When they reached the station, Garcia had already escorted Susie inside and put her in an interrogation room. Carl, all bright-eyed and bouncy, led Amber into the tiny room attached to the one Susie now occupied.

"Isn't this exciting?" Carl whisper-hissed at her once they were closed in the small, dark room. "We're gonna watch the boss interrogating a perp!"

Amber tried to smile at his enthusiasm, but her stomach was in knots. Susie sat in the room alone, hands clasped on top of the plain Formica table. Susie had stopped crying, though her eyes were still red. She sniffled occasionally. Amber watched as her foot idly tapped out an uneven rhythm on the floor.

The door to the main room opened and both Amber and Susie glanced that way. Chief Brown walked in. Shortly after, Amber and Carl were joined by Garcia.

Questions started out simple. "How did you know Melanie?" and "Were you close with Whitney?" and "Did you know about the affair?"

But soon enough, the chief was pushing her with more complicated questions. Namely, why had she not told police that it had been *she* who took Sydney to school the morning of Melanie's death? Why, if she knew Whitney's alibi was a lie, had she never corrected anyone? Susie was quiet or evasive when it came to that question, so the chief would back off and circle back. But eventually he pushed, not accepting her vague answers. He pushed and pushed.

"Because I was scared *I* killed her, okay?" Susie finally snapped, swiping under her eyes quickly. Angrily. "Because … to go to the police, I'd have to admit I'd been poisoning her. That's still a crime even if it's not murder."

"It is," the chief agreed.

"I was scared," Susie said, sniffing.

"And you poisoned her to make her sick enough to step down as head of the committee?"

Susie pursed her lips. "It sounds so bad when you word it like that."

"That's because it *is* bad, Miss Paulson. I shouldn't have to tell you this isn't the way to get what you want."

"Don't lecture me," Susie said, crossing her arms. "You don't know how much I've given to this town. You've only been here a few years. You don't get to judge me."

"You're right," he said. "Judging you isn't my job. I just need the facts." He paused. "I get that you were scared, but why did you trust Whitney Sadler to have your best interest at heart?"

"Well, I mean, she was just as involved with this as I was and I was in hysterics when I found out Melanie was dead. Whitney … she said she was going to take care of it. Clean up my mess because I'd taken our plan too far. She made it seem like she was doing me a favor. That we were in this together."

Though the chief's back was to Amber, she imagined him cocking a brow at Susie in disbelief.

"Where did you get the ethylene glycol you were adding to Melanie's tea?"

Susie squirmed. "Whitney."

Amber pursed her lips.

"She was in med school before she got pregnant with Sydney," Susie said. "She said she had a knack for pharmacology so she knew of just the thing to give Melanie that could make her sick without killing her. She just ..." Susie swallowed. "The last batch she had must have been too much. Tipped the scales too far in the other direction. Whitney helped make it look accidental so we wouldn't get caught. It was just a really stupid plan that got out of hand."

The chief paused long enough that it made Susie squirm again. "Melanie had a thousand times the amount of ethylene glycol in her system that she would have had from a small diluted dose mixed into her tea."

Amber watched as understanding came over Susie's face. Her creased brow smoothed out, her eyes widened, her mouth dropped open. "I ... I *didn't* kill her?"

"Not unless you injected a syringe full of ethylene glycol into her neck."

"Her *neck*?" Susie put a hand over her mouth. "I don't even know where to get that stuff. I've never used a syringe before. I didn't *do* that. It wasn't me. I swear it."

"Okay, okay, calm down," he said, both hands out, fingers splayed, to placate her. "Where was Whitney getting her supply?"

Susie sat up straighter, wide eyes darting this way and that, not focusing on anything in particular. "I don't know. The day of the town hall, when I found out Melanie got the director job over me ... I was pissed. I was smoking in the parking lot, trying to calm down, and Whitney-freaking-Sadler walked up and asked to bum a cigarette. This woman had hardly acknowledged my existence before this, mind you, but I was too pissed off to think about it too hard."

Susie was on a roll now that suspicion seemed to have shifted away from her.

"So she and I started talking about how much we both hated Melanie." Susie winced then, as if she only just now realized how horrible she sounded. "I didn't hate her. I just hated that she took the spot from me. *I* deserved it." When the chief didn't offer her words of sympathy, she continued. "Whitney was pissed that Melanie not only hooked up with her husband, but then showed up twelve years later and weaseled her way into life here, including the Here and Meow."

"And that's when you came up with your plan to poison her?"

Susie absently scratched at her elbow. "Basically, yeah. I said it was too bad we couldn't get rid of her so she could stop ruining our lives. Whitney was like, 'What if we can?'"

Amber wanted to launch herself through the two-way mirror so she could wring Susie's neck. Then she'd find Whitney and wring hers too.

"I swear the plan wasn't to kill her. It was just to make her sick and drop out."

"Do you have any idea why the plan changed?" the chief asked.

Susie shook her head. "I swear I thought it was a horrible accident this whole time. I don't know why Whitney would … why she'd *inject* Melanie."

"Okay. Sit tight. I'll be right back."

Ten seconds later, Chief Brown had joined Amber, Carl,

and Garcia in the small room attached to the interrogation room Susie still sat in. Amber glanced over to see the other woman beyond the thick, dark glass, staring off into space.

"Carl, do you have those phone records ready?" the chief asked.

"Yes, boss, they're in room four."

"Amber? I've got something I need you to see."

She followed him out of the interrogation room, past the door that hid Susie from view, and down the hallway. The sad-looking lobby with its mismatched chairs was empty. He let her inside the closet-sized room he'd first questioned her in and shut the door.

A beige file folder lay on the table.

Once they were both seated, he said, "I have Melanie's phone records here." He patted the folder. "You were her closest friend in town. How long was this relationship with Derrick going on? Someone says it only started in the last six months, someone else says it's been going on since she moved here. Others say it never officially ended twelve years ago and the affair's been happening all along."

Amber was almost positive it wasn't the last one.

She scanned the chief's face. The bags were still dark beneath his eyes. He was desperate to solve this and get some rest. And that's what she saw in his expression now—desperation. Something he wanted to tell her but was holding back.

Gathering up her magic in her core, she reached across the table and placed a hand on his forearm. The thought-reveal spell came easily.

His last thought came unbidden, without Amber needing

to ask a question to pull the answer out of him. She yanked her hand away, clutching it with her other one and holding both to her chest.

"What did you see?" he asked, a thread of hope laced into his tone.

"Melanie was pregnant."

The chief stared at her dumbly, clearly still impressed with her "psychic" skill. "Every time I wonder if I've made the right choice in including you, you do something to prove I did."

Amber didn't know what to say to that. Her gaze flicked to the beige file folder of its own accord.

Without a word, the chief nudged it toward her.

She flipped it open. There were pages and pages of messages. Messages that clearly showed Derrick and Melanie had started communicating just days after Melanie had moved to Edgehill. After several of those, there were a few pages of what looked like credit card statements.

Amber looked up, confused.

"This is only the tip of the iceberg. Derrick was right that they only saw each other when they could, but that was fairly frequently. Whitney travels a lot; his daughter is in boarding school an hour away ..."

Amber recalled the pictures she'd seen on Whitney's social media pages. Her by the pool or on a beach or playing on a tennis court. Derrick had never been in a single picture.

"That number, though, isn't one registered to Derrick on his family plan with Whitney," he said. "But after sifting through his credit card statements, we found the purchase of another phone. We've confirmed this number belongs to Derrick." He pointed at the stack of papers. "Flip to the back."

Amber did as she was told and stopped on the last page. It was a series of messages sent the evening before Melanie's death.

> *5:15PM: You still going to your friend's house tonight?*
>
> *6:20PM: I'm feeling kind of crappy still, but do you want to swing by here on your way?* ☺
>
> *6:22PM: Hello?*
>
> *6:24PM: I really need to talk to you, actually. You were supposed to call me back days ago …*
>
> *7:41PM: This would be better in person.*
>
> *7:43PM: Derrick?????*
>
> *7:45PM: Seriously … I need to talk.*
>
> *8:01PM: Ugh, I feel really awful again. Sometimes I can barely get off the couch … I'm so weak. I can't figure out what's wrong with me. Maybe I can get one of Amber's magical heal-alls tomorrow.*
>
> *8:10PM: … Derrick?*
>
> *8:15PM: Fine … maybe this will get you to call me. I'm pregnant, okay? And I'm keeping it. What do you want to do?*
>
> *9:10PM: Why aren't you answering my calls either?*
>
> *9:18PM: Nevermind. Susie just showed up with a care package for me … she's making me tea right now. That's what a caring person does, Derrick. If you're ghosting*

*me now because things have gotten too real with us in
the last couple months, I'm really disappointed. You're
better than this.*

*9:46PM: I'm sorry I said all that, babe. I'm just scared.
Please call me, okay? Even if it's not until the morning.
I love you.*

That was her last message.

Once Amber got over the gut-punch reality that two had
died that day, what she'd just read caught up with her. "Derrick
doesn't know about the pregnancy. He said he would have left
Whitney for her if she asked. He surely would have if he had
known Melanie was pregnant, wouldn't he?"

The chief nodded. "I was thinking that, too. But we searched
that house top to bottom. No sign of this other phone and
Derrick claims he doesn't know where it is. I didn't break the
pregnancy news. That's a can of worms I don't need opened
right now."

Derrick had claimed messages from Melanie just suddenly dried up, that she abruptly stopped answering his texts
and calls.

Amber scanned the messages again. "What if he never saw
them? What if Whitney found the phone? What if *this*—" she
tapped the sheet of messages with a finger "—is what sent
Whitney over the edge?"

"It's very possible," he said. "We need to get Whitney in
here for questioning again."

Amber's mind whirred. If Whitney had known about not
only the affair, but the pregnancy before Melanie died, then

that public display Henrietta Bishop had seen play out on the Sadlers' lawn had all been an act on Whitney's part. And then she had thrown Susie under the bus.

Amber wondered if it had been Whitney's idea to put the vial from Amber's shop in Melanie's hand, just so she could take Amber down too. At least for a little while.

The bubbling anger returned, churning in Amber's gut. Her magic reacted in time, pulsing under her skin.

"Can I talk to Susie?" she asked.

The chief squinted at her. "About what?"

"Whitney isn't going to confess to anything," Amber said. "She's put in too much work already to deflect blame. But she'll talk to Susie."

Before the chief could get his next question out, she pulled the recording device out of her purse. She'd yet to return it to sour-faced Dolores. "Think she'd be willing to give this thing a spin?"

The chief smiled. "Let's go find out."

CHAPTER 17

Amber strode into the interrogation room with the device in her hands. Susie gave a start. Her gaze shifted from the device to Amber's face and back again.

"What are you doing here?"

The chief walked in after her and shut the door. "Miss Blackwood is a consultant on the case."

Susie sputtered a laugh. "*Her?*"

"You're really going to pass judgement right now when you poisoned a woman so you could head a cat festival?" Amber snapped.

That shut Susie up.

Amber then proceeded to tell Susie about the text messages, the pregnancy, and their theory that Whitney had killed Melanie.

Susie grew paler and paler. She crossed her arms tight across her body. "And she ... she called the station to say this was all *my* idea? She wanted to let me take the fall for it all?"

"Yep," Amber said.

Susie's jaw clenched.

"We have a proposal for you," the chief said.

Amber placed the device on the counter.

The chief said, "Would you be willing to wear that and—"

Susie stood, pulling her button-down shirt free from where it was tucked into her black slacks. "Let's take her down."

Chief Brown, Garcia, Carl, and Amber piled into the chief's cruiser and followed Susie to Whitney's house. They parked at the same curb where Amber had idled only yesterday. Susie turned onto American Curl without them.

Once they were situated, the chief set up the equipment in the car so they could both record and listen in on Susie's conversation with Whitney. The device hadn't been turned on yet, so they stared at a blank laptop screen, the program primed and ready once Susie went live.

Five minutes later, a green line spiked on the screen, capturing the sound of Susie's clothes as they rubbed against the tiny microphone. Then the sound settled and Susie's semi-frantic breaths filled the car.

"Okay, I think I'm ready," came Susie's voice loud and clear. "Can you hear me okay?"

Amber texted her a thumbs-up icon.

"Cool. Here I go," Susie said. "I feel like James Bond or something."

The chief snorted. Carl cackled so loud it shook the car. Amber chewed on her thumbnail, eyes glued to the screen. She wasn't sure why the jumping green lines comforted her, but they did.

After several long, agonizing seconds, Amber heard the sound of knuckles on wood.

"Here she comes," Susie whispered.

Amber hoped the woman wasn't so caught up in being James Bond that she made it painfully obvious she was up to something.

"Oh!" said Whitney. "Hi, Sooz. I didn't … uh … what are you doing here?"

"We need to talk."

Something was jostled and Amber imagined Susie barging her way into Whitney's house, bumping into the blonde as she did.

"What about?" Whitney asked. The door closed.

"Want to know where I just came from?"

Whitney audibly sighed. "I don't really have time for guessing games, Susie."

"Are you going somewhere?" Susie asked. "This seems like a lot of luggage."

Amber and the chief shared a look. He started the car and crept onto American Curl Avenue, parking several houses down from where Susie's little white four-door sat at the curb.

"Not that it's any of your business," Whitney said, "but I'm thinking of taking Sydney on a little trip. She doesn't know about the divorce yet, so I want to break the news to her gently."

"I drove here straight from the police station," Susie said. "Any guesses why?"

Whitney sighed again. "If you're going to talk in questions, you can just leave now."

"I got called in for questioning because *you* called the station to tell them I was the one who masterminded this whole poisoning scheme," Susie snapped.

"Well, it *was* your idea, Susie."

"It was a joke to blow off steam because I was pissed. You're the one who got the ethylene glycol. You're the one who suggested I add it to her tea. You're the one who told me the best amount to use and how often."

Whitney scoffed. "I didn't exactly put a gun to your head. You *wanted* to do it."

"I didn't want to kill her."

"Yeah, well, accidents happen."

Footsteps echoed away from Susie. Amber pictured Whitney shrugging after calling Melanie's death an accident and walking into the kitchen. Susie clomped after her.

"That's just it," Susie said. "It wasn't an accident. I saw a tox report. There was way more in her system than she'd have if she just ingested some from a drink. I didn't put that much in her tea."

"Well, neither did I," Whitney said. "Guess we're at a stalemate. And the police clearly let you go, so I don't know why you're here harassing me on the hardest day of my life."

Amber fought an eye roll.

"Because I wanted to give you the chance to tell me what actually happened before I tell them what *I* think happened," Susie said.

"You were just there. Why didn't you tell them then and save us both the trouble? Oh, because then you'd be in the psych ward instead of my kitchen. Because that's where you belong, Sooz. In the psych ward. You're *crazy.*"

"I'm not crazy," she snapped.

"You are!" Whitney laughed. "Look at you. You're sweaty and pale."

"Because I was just questioned for a murder I didn't commit! You and I were supposed to be a team in this. Mel would get sick. I'd get her position and you'd get the satisfaction of knowing you took her down a peg for hooking up with Derrick all those years ago. When she came here, she screwed things up for both of us."

"She deserved worse than what she got," Whitney muttered so low, Amber almost didn't catch it.

"What was that?" Susie said.

Whitney paused for so long, Amber worried something had gone wrong. Then, quietly, Whitney said, "He was going to leave me for her, you know?"

"What?" Susie asked, sounding genuinely surprised. Whitney wasn't the only actor in that room. "Why? Melanie didn't mean anything to him. She couldn't have."

"She was *pregnant*."

Susie gasped appropriately. "How did you even find that out?"

"That night he was going over to his friend's house in Belhaven? He was in the shower and I needed to get something out of his office. Something started buzzing in one of the drawers. Over and over," Whitney said. "It was a phone I'd never seen before. Kind of cheap looking. Easily disposable, I guess. There were all these messages from a woman who was clearly trying to get a hold of him. She used winky faces." Amber imagined Whitney rolling her eyes. "The number looked familiar, so I cross-checked it in my own phone and guess who it was …"

"Melanie," Susie said, an air of disgust in her tone that Amber wasn't sure was fake.

"When he got out of the shower, I asked him if there was anything he needed to tell me. We got into this huge fight. I didn't even mention the phone. I don't know what I was planning to do with it. Derrick took off. And then there I was with the phone. Staring at it while messages came in, one after the other. She called it at one point and … oh, I almost answered it. Almost. But I liked the idea of her being in pain and alone and him ignoring her. So I let it go to voicemail."

Amber's stomach was a mess. She wasn't sure how much more she could listen to.

"And then she broke the news in a text. In a text! Told *my* husband that she was pregnant and I just …"

Susie audibly swallowed. "What happened? We can come up with a story together to tell the police. Something that keeps us both from getting arrested for this. I didn't know how bad things had gotten for you."

"I snapped, Sooz," Whitney said softly. "I swear I saw red. I know a guy from back in my med school days who works in a lab. I asked him if I could come see him; he knows how upset I was when I had to drop out. When he ran out to get us some lunch, I stole a syringe and some more ethylene glycol.

"After you left Melanie in the morning, I went over there but she wasn't home, so I let myself in the back. I didn't go there with a plan, not really. But then she got home and just seeing her set something off in me. When she headed for the bedroom where I was hiding, it was like I left my body. I

236

don't even remember slipping the needle into her neck. But the next thing I knew, she was on the ground …"

Tears streamed down Amber's face, a fist pressed hard to her mouth.

"I'm scared, Sooz," she said. "That's why I called the police. I have a daughter to worry about. Someone who relies on me. You don't have a family, so something like this won't be as hard on you. If they think it was all you and it was an accident, they'll be more lenient. Maybe a year or two and it'll likely be reduced to six months for good behavior."

Amber could have sworn she heard Susie's frantic heartbeat.

"We're talking about jail time," Susie said. "For something I didn't do."

Whitney groaned. "We just went through all this! You were already actively poisoning her. You're not exactly innocent here. Melanie deserved it. You know that. She's been a blight on Edgehill since she got here. I did us both a favor."

Something scooted across the floor. A chair, maybe? Had they been sitting around the dining room table?

"Sorry, Whitney, I can't take the fall for you," Susie said, her footsteps heavy and quick.

The men in the car all tensed. The chief unhooked his seatbelt. They were all poised and ready. Amber's heart thundered in time to Susie's footfalls.

"Sooz! Where are you going?" Whitney called out. "We can think of something else … Susan!"

And then there was a second set of footfalls, a groan, and a crash.

All four doors of the cop car opened and the men were

sprinting down the sidewalk before Amber had gotten out of the car. She ran after them, worried they wouldn't get there before Whitney Sadler killed someone else.

By the time Amber ran up the porch steps to the Sadler home, the door was open. Carl was tending to Susie, who was sitting in the entryway, a gash on her forehead and the remnants of a shattered vase nearby.

A thud sounded from somewhere deep in the house and Amber went tearing off after the sound. She came to a skidding halt when she found Whitney facedown on the floor in the kitchen, hands held behind her by Chief Brown. A bloodied knife lay on the floor and Garcia stood a couple feet away with a gash slashed through his arm.

"You okay?" she asked.

"I'll live," he said gruffly, though he was smiling. They were the first words she'd heard him utter.

The chief looked over at Amber, who stood heaving by the counter island in the middle of the kitchen. He nodded. She nodded back.

The two officers then hauled Whitney, handcuffed, to her feet. They read her her Miranda Rights. Whitney didn't so much as look at Amber as they walked by, Whitney's head hung low. Amber watched them descend the steps and then turn left down the sidewalk to the awaiting police car.

Carl helped Susie to her feet. And, despite her being a victim in this case, Carl officially arrested Susie, too.

"I can get home on my own," Amber said. "That car's going to be packed."

Susie let herself be escorted toward the door, but then

stopped, causing Carl to bump into her. She glanced around Carl to Amber. "For what it's worth, I'm sorry."

Amber couldn't get herself to accept the apology, so she said nothing. When Susie's shoulders slumped, Carl led her out of the house.

As the police car zipped past, Susie's car still sitting at the curb, Amber closed the door to Whitney's house and slowly walked down the stairs. She knew now what had happened to her friend, but the hole in her heart was still there. She knew it would take a long time to heal.

She took her time walking home, reliving the good times she'd had with Melanie. The movie marathons and game nights around her dining room table. How she and Melanie had laughed so hard they cried.

Amber hoped that wherever Melanie was now, there was laughter there too.

EPILOGUE

News of Whitney Sadler being Melanie's murderer, with Susie Paulson as her accomplice, was the biggest scandal to hit Edgehill since … well, no one could remember a bigger story. People Amber hadn't spoken to since high school flooded into the Quirky Whisker offering their condolences.

Amber suspected it was a little bit out of guilt too, as she was sure at least a third of Edgehill's population had suspected her at some point.

Amber and Nicolette worked to get Melanie's house cleaned out. Kimberly Jones and Jack Terrence swung by to help or to bring food.

A funeral was held a week later, and it seemed the whole of Edgehill showed up to pay their respects. At the cemetery, Amber spotted a wrecked-looking Derrick Sadler standing a ways off from the crowd, hands shoved in his pockets, shoulders hunched. Amber wondered what life would look like for little Sydney now.

A day later, Nicolette was gone. Amber was sad to see her go. She was the last piece of Melanie that Amber had.

Slowly, life got back to normal. The Here and Meow festival crept ever closer.

Orders for Amber's animated toys poured in at such a

rapid speed, she wasn't sure she could keep up. She worked late into the night for weeks on end, moving her production headquarters downstairs as plastic pieces and half-formed spells and toys had started taking over every square inch of space in her tiny apartment.

One evening, she had a dozen cat toys lined up on a table in the middle of the room, all fitted with her newly perfected magic-infused discs that allowed the cats to run as well as walk. For some reason, though, one out of every ten or so glitched, which often resulted in a sprinting plastic cat darting around the room, tormenting her live cats.

Amber wasn't sure if Tom would ever forgive her for the plastic calico who sprinted toward him at full speed, which he only narrowly escaped by jumping onto the window bench seat. The calico, with no spatial awareness, slammed directly into the wall and shattered into hundreds of tiny pieces. Even now, weeks later, she still found little calico pieces scattered around the apartment.

Now she stood in her dark shop, several quietly waiting plastic cats sitting before her in two neat rows. To help speed up her process, and to weed out the glitchy ones, she had taken to activating large numbers of the toys at once.

Glancing at the troubleshoot spell written in her grimoire lying open on the table beside a black-and-white cat she'd modeled after Alley, Amber muttered the incantation and then swept her hand over the area above the cats' heads. At once, they came to life. Some scratched at their ears with a back foot, some licked plastic paws with their pink plastic tongues, and others stretched, backs arched and tails hoisted in the air.

Amber smiled at them, proud that she'd created a good batch this time.

Then one of the cats, an all-white one with blue eyes, silently roared like a lion and started running, launching itself off the end of the table as if it thought it could fly. Amber wasn't sure why some seemed to develop their own personalities almost immediately. Any little slip in her attention or intention while fusing magic into the discs that filled their bodies could result in rogue animals.

She called on her magic to halt the cat in midair and brought it back to the table. It bucked and thrashed. Amber quickly muttered a deactivation spell to stop it.

Something shifted in her peripheral vision and her gaze snapped to the glass doors of her shop. It was nearly ten in the evening on a Tuesday. Russian Blue Avenue was like a ghost town after eight, and usually sooner.

The familiar shape of Chief Owen Brown stood outside, his eyes wide.

Before she could think of what to say or do, he quickly walked away.

Amber's heart thundered in her chest.

He must have seen everything.

He knew she was a witch.

She had a feeling that her very precarious alliance with the chief had just ended. The man who had spent almost his entire time in Edgehill suspicious of her, now knew her biggest secret.

Thank you for reading *Pawsitively Poisonous*! If you enjoyed this story, please consider leaving a review. Reviews mean the world to authors. Reviews often mean more sales, and more sales means more freedom to write more books.

Continue the series with:

Pawsitively Cursed

Pawsitively Secretive

Pawsitively Swindled

Pawsitively Betrayed

Other books by Melissa Erin Jackson:

If you're looking for a slightly darker tale, consider *The Forgotten Child*, a haunting paranormal mystery starring a reluctant medium.

The dead can speak. They need her to listen.

Ever since Riley Thomas, reluctant medium extraordinaire, accidentally released a malevolent spirit from a

Ouija board when she was thirteen, she's taken a hard pass on scary movies, haunted houses, and cemeteries. Twelve years later, when her best friend pressures her into spending a paranormal investigation weekend at the infamous Jordanville Ranch—former home of deceased serial killer Orin Jacobs—Riley's *still* not ready to accept the fact that she can communicate with ghosts.

Shortly after their arrival at the ranch, the spirit of a little boy contacts Riley; a child who went missing—and was never found—in 1973.

In order to put the young boy's spirit to rest, she has to come to grips with her ability. But how can she solve a mystery that happened a decade before she was born? Especially when someone who knows Orin's secrets wants to keep the truth buried—no matter the cost.

Available at Amazon, Kobo, Barnes & Noble, and iBooks. Now available as an audiobook, too!

Acknowledgements

This book wouldn't have even reached the idea stage if it hadn't been for Kyla Gardner and Margarita Martinez. Thank you to you both for "forcing" me into the cozy mystery genre. Now I never want to leave!

I must thank all my early readers who helped my panicked-self navigate this new genre I've only just dipped my toes into. Thank you, Mom, Krista Hall, Brandon Moore, Christiane Loeffler, Jennifer Laam, Garrett Lemons, Lindsey Duga, Tristin Milazzo, Julianna Taylor, Malik Lockhart, Jacynthia West, Jasmine Warren, and Kara Klemcke. And thanks to Courtney Hanson simply for being the best dang cheerleader ever. SSDGM, girl.

Thank you again (and again and again!) to Maggie Hall for these gorgeous covers. Working with you is always so fun and I'm constantly floored by how talented you are.

Thanks once again to Michelle Raymond for the formatting help. And for all the cats! The extra little touches are even better than I hoped for!

Thank you to Justin Cohen for being such a great nitpicky

proofreader. I look forward to working with you on many books to come!

Victoria! I'm very excited to be working with you on the audiobooks. It's always a little strange to hear your on words read back to you, but you've made the process so easy. Thank you for helping bring Amber to life.

Socrates, Dusty, and Racket—you've been a great source of feline inspiration. RIP, Odum. I'm not saying you were the inspiration behind Savannah the Maine Coon, but I'm not *not* saying that either.

And, finally, thank you to Sam for keeping me sane. Thank you for doing the dishes and the laundry, for taking care of the animals (why do we have so many dogs?!), and making late night snack and Red Bull runs so I can keep writing. You're my favorite and I love you to bits.

About the Author

Melissa has had a love of stories for as long as she can remember, but only started penning her own during her freshman year of college. She majored in Wildlife, Fish, and Conservation Biology at UCDavis. Yet, while she was neck-deep in organic chemistry and physics, she kept finding herself writing stories in the back of the classroom about fairies and trolls and magic. She finished her degree, but it never captured her heart the way writing did.

Now she owns her own dog walking business (that's sort of wildlife related, right?) by day … and afternoon and night … and writes whenever she gets a spare moment. The Microsoft Word app is a gift from the gods!

She alternates mostly between fantasy and mystery (often with a paranormal twist). All her books have some element of "other" to them … witches, ghosts, UFOs. There's no better way to escape the real world than getting lost in a fictional one.

She lives in Northern California with her very patient boyfriend and way too many pets.

Melissa Erin Jackson

Her debut novel, *The Forgotten Child*, released in October of 2018. She is currently fast at work writing both the Riley Thomas mystery series, and the Witch of Edgehill series.

You can find out more at: https://melissajacksonbooks.com